GOALIE
INTERFERENCE

NHL SCORPIONS, BOOK #2

Nikki Worrell

Cover design by David Goldhahn (www.davidgoldhahn.com)

Editing by Madison Seidler (http://www.madisonseidler.com)

Interior Design by Angela McLaurin
(https://www.facebook.com/FictionalFormats)

Also by Nikki Worrell
Stories For Amanda - October 2013
The Enforcer (NHL Scorpions Book #1) - May 2013

Table of Contents

Dedication

My first book, *The Enforcer*, was dedicated to the NHL's enforcers. This book is dedicated to all of the people who took a chance on me and read that book. Unless you've tried to write a book before, I don't think you can truly understand how grateful new authors are for readers taking a chance on them. I was overwhelmed by the mostly positive reviews and support from you all, so I thank you allowing me to entertain you. Vlad and Zoe's story was written with your entertainment in mind!

Glossary of Hockey Terms

5-hole: The area right between the goalie's legs.

Butterfly Goalie: A style of goaltending distinguished by the way the goalie quickly drops to his knees in order to guard the lower part of the net.

Checking: Using the hip or body to knock an opponent against the boards or to the ice.

Cross Check: penalty by checking an opponent with the stick held in both hands, rather than using a hip or body, possibly causing injury.

Crease: The blue area directly in front of the net, extending six feet in front of the net and one foot outside of each goal post.

Faceoff: The method used to begin play. One player from each team fights for the puck as the official drops it to start the play

LTIR: Long Term Injured Reserve

Major Penalty: Five-minute penalty.

Minor Penalty: Two-minute penalty.

Poke Check: Poking the puck away with the stick.

Power Play: Results in the one team losing a player for two minutes or more, giving the other team an advantage to score.

Trapezoid (Trap): Area behind the goalie's net (behind goal line) where the goalie can play the puck. This is the only area behind the goal line that the goalie can play the puck without receiving a penalty.

War Room: Office in Toronto where video is sent to review a questionable goal.

Prologue

Two years ago …

Vlad Bejsiuk, a Ukrainian goalie for the NHL's San Diego Scorpions, was on his way to see the doctor. Periodic therapy sessions with the team's sports psychologist were mandatory for the players, which was the *only* reason he was standing outside Dr. Zoe Millis's door.

He had put off going for as long as he could. Therapy sessions were the bane of his existence. It took him over a year to get used to Dr. Phillips, and then she quit, mid-season, to become a stay-at-home mom. He was happy for her, but he didn't like change.

Dr. Millis's office was in her house, instead of at the rink where he had previously gone for his sessions. Taking a calming breath, he raised his hand to push the doorbell. Before he actually hit it, he got a look at the new doctor through the glass.

Nice …

The first thing he noticed was a faint pink streak in her pixie-cropped hair. She was on the short side, which he loved. Her arms were toned, and her ass looked incredible in jeans that hugged her like a second skin. His eyes took in all of those details in the quick peek he got of her as she walked into the hallway and bent down to pick something up off the floor.

When she stood back up, Vlad got a nice view of her head on. She jumped back, surprised, throwing her hand over her heart when she saw him standing on the other side of the door. He still couldn't seem to make himself push the doorbell.

As she walked toward him, he checked her out further. Her breasts were small and fit her petite frame perfectly. Vlad was more of an ass guy anyway. He forced himself to stop ogling her and pasted on what he hoped passed as a friendly smile.

When Zoe saw a man standing at her door, staring at her, her heart just about jumped out of her chest. It took her a second to recognize the Scorpions' goalie. The only times she'd seen his face were when he was being interviewed after a game. Other than that, he had his goalie mask on, so he wasn't as immediately recognizable as some of the other players.

Since she had noticed the way he checked her out, Zoe thought it might be a good idea to establish professional boundaries with him right from the start. She gave him a slight smile as she opened the door and introduced herself, "Hi, I'm Dr. Millis."

Vlad shook her hand as he took a step toward her. "Zoe, right?"

Keeping her smile intact, she said, "Let's stick to Dr. Millis for now. Come on in, and we'll get started." Zoe led the way through her kitchen to the rear of the house where her office was located. "Have a seat, Vlad."

"I think we can stick to Mr. Bejsiuk for now."

Zoe's smile was real when she responded, "Touché, Mr. Bejsiuk. I didn't mean to offend you; I just like to keep a professional relationship with my clients." That actually wasn't true. The truth was that Zoe hated being stuffy, but she was taught in school to keep a professional distance from all clients. Be nice, but not overly friendly; caring, but not to the point of emotional attachment. She was starting to think that approach might not work for her. Maybe it was because she was working with athletes. They were pretty laid back for the most part and treated everyone like a buddy. She quickly got the idea that she could use Vlad to experiment on; to try a new approach of interacting with her clients that was less formal, but still professional.

As they took their seats, Zoe noticed how much he filled his. She knew his stats said he was six-foot- one, and two hundred ten pounds. His stats did not mention how his dark, wavy hair was just long enough to charmingly curl over the top of his collar. They also didn't mention his captivating light brown eyes. He had quite a few laugh lines there, as well, which only added to his allure—and alluring he was.

Clearing her mind of those thoughts, Zoe started their session by asking Vlad how he felt the season was going. He had one of the best records in the league that year and seemed like he was happy and healthy.

3

"My win record can tell you how the season's going. I'm having a hell of a year. Of course I'm not taking all the credit; our defense is the main reason for that. The team's hot so far. I don't have any issues to talk about yet. I'm only here for my periodic, mandatory session to meet the new shrink." He winked at her, trying to get her on a more personal level.

"Fair enough," Zoe said. "How about if you tell me a little about yourself? I'd like to get to know you." Zoe knew the basics, but she purposefully stayed away from the sports pages and gossip rags. She'd rather form her own opinion directly from the source. "From your name and your accent, is it safe to assume that you're Russian?" His accent was slight, but could still be detected. It was more than a bit sexy, and she wanted to hear him speak some more.

"Close. I'm actually from the Ukraine. I do speak Russian, though, since I'm from the South. Most of the people in Southern and Eastern Ukraine speak Russian. The rest speak Ukrainian, but the languages are very similar. Russian is a bit more … polished, I guess." A lot of people lumped the Ukraine in with Russia. The people looked the same and sounded the same to outsiders.

"Your accent is so slight. Most of the Russians or Ukrainians in the NHL can be hard to understand. Where did you learn to speak English?" Zoe had always been impressed with people who were proficient in more than one language.

"My mother is English, and my father is Ukrainian. I learned both languages growing up. It wasn't hard because I was taught both from the time I was born." Vlad didn't think he could have spoken two languages if he hadn't been taught from birth. A scholar, he was not. Thank God he was good at hockey. "How about you Zoe? Where do you come from?"

Zoe noticed he didn't call her Dr. Millis, but she let it go. "My parents were both from Maine. Both Heinz 57 varieties, so that makes me quite a mix. Mostly Irish, I guess. Some English, Scottish, German ..." Zoe trailed off with a wave of her hand.

"Were? Where are they now?" He couldn't imagine that she'd lost both her parents. She couldn't be more than thirty.

"Both of my parents died when I was thirteen. My father was an adrenaline junkie, and he died parachuting. My mother was already sick with cancer and died eight months after he did." Zoe still didn't like talking about it. It had been a little over fifteen years since she'd lost her parents, but some days it still felt like yesterday. They had been a close family. She still had her brother, Aidan, though. Thankfully, he moved to San Diego with her when she got the job with the Scorpions.

Vlad was appalled. "Wow, that's rough. I'm really sorry, Zoe. Who raised you after that?"

Zoe thought about telling him the rest of her story, but she could see that this session was getting a bit off track. "Another family member. In any case, let's get back to you. Is there anything you'd like to accomplish that you haven't yet in your career?"

Vlad was enjoying getting to know Zoe, and he frowned. "Okay, so I guess we're done talking about you." Sighing, he continued, "Well, obviously I'd like to win the Cup before I retire. I'm already thirty-six, and there are tons of young guns coming up through the ranks. I can't say it's not intimidating."

"Are you starting to think about retirement?"

Vlad laughed. "Good God, no. Not right now anyway. I'm at the top of my game; it's just something that's in the far back of my mind. At the end of the day, my hips are sore, and my groin, well, being a goalie is particularly tough on those areas."

"I can't possibly imagine how you feel after a game. I'm a runner, and I'm already starting to feel some aches and pains that I didn't used to have. I'm only twenty-nine, but there's a difference already from when I was twenty. Time catches us all, I suppose." Zoe had always loved to run. She started in high school, lettering in track, and she never looked back. She'd even completed a couple of marathons.

"It's all good for now. I can deal with some aches and pains. The pros far outweigh the cons." He couldn't imagine doing anything else. Hockey was his life.

Zoe glanced at the clock and was surprised to see that their session was over. "Well, Vlad, it was a pleasure meeting you. You'll be happy to know that you survived your first mandatory session." Zoe gave him a smile and got up to show him out.

When they got to the door, Vlad took her hand in both of his. "It was great meeting you too, Zoe. I don't like having to come to these sessions, but I think you may make it a bit more bearable for me." He rubbed his thumb over the back of her hand and took his time releasing it before he walked out the door.

Chapter 1

Present day ...

She was going to kill him. Dead. Put a nail in his coffin, never to be heard from again, dead!

Zoe knew that Vlad had a major thing for her. Hell, she had a thing for him, too, but she also knew that it wasn't possible for them to date. The rules were very clearly stated. The team psychologist was not to have a personal relationship with any of her clients. No exceptions.

For two years Vlad had dogged her, trying to take down her walls, to make her simply go with her feelings. He knew she wanted him as badly as he did her. He tried to assure her they could keep it a secret so she wouldn't lose her job, but unfortunately, the girl had morals.

Vlad was all about doing the right thing. He helped old ladies cross the street, stopped the kids next door from bullying their little brother, and gave to the ASPCA. But there were some things that didn't fit neatly into the parameters of good morals. One of those things was being in love with someone who was off limits.

At first, Vlad just thought he'd like to take her for a quick tangle in his sheets. He dreamed about her ass, which would more than fill his hands, and her runner's legs that could easily wrap around him, pulling him in close. As he got to know her, though, he realized it was much more than that. It freaked him out for a while, but as he watched his best friend, former Scorpions' enforcer, fall in love, he became less and less freaked out. Jody LaGrange had married his soul mate that very night and was happier than Vlad had ever seen him. He wanted that, too—with Zoe.

Scaring away her dates was frighteningly easy and became somewhat of a game for Vlad. They didn't even question her when Vlad made his outrageous comments in front of them, and she should be glad they were taking off. Obviously they didn't think enough of her to give her the benefit of the doubt, so they didn't deserve her anyway. Where were his thanks?

"Oh my God, Vlad," Zoe said as her wedding date excused himself with the lame excuse of having to let his dog out. "What the fuck? You have to stop doing this! You can't interfere with every date I have."

Vlad poked her in the chest and said, "You should be *thanking* me. What kind of a man doesn't even try to defend his date when I tell him you might have some kind of STD?" At the look on her face, he took a step back, putting his hands up in the air, palms forward. "I admit, I might have stepped over the line this time, I do, but still, he just isn't the one for you."

"Vlad, you told him I might need to be checked out because *your* last date told you she might have something. Don't you get it? You just told him that we've slept together. Why do you hate me all of the sudden? Why are you saying these things about me? Not only is it obnoxious, but you could cost me my job if the wrong person overheard you! It's a pretty crappy way to treat a friend."

Vlad didn't know what to say to that, because she was right. The entire thing was fabricated. And she definitely had a point about someone overhearing him. It *was* a crappy way to treat a friend, but he didn't know what else to do. He couldn't stand to see her with other men. Short of quitting the team, he couldn't see a way to convince her that they could be together. Admittedly, ruining her dates was probably not the best way to go about it.

Vlad ran a hand over his face and let out a gusty sigh. "You're right, Zoe. Shit, I'm sorry. I'm just running out of ways to convince you to take a chance on us."

Softening somewhat, Zoe looked him in the eye. "Come on, Vlad. You know it's not a matter of me not wanting to take a chance on you. I've worked hard in my career. This is a great job for me, and I love what I do. Please, stop pursuing me. It's hard enough trying to force myself to ignore these feelings for you on a daily basis. Stop making it harder. Please. Can you do that for me?"

Out of the corner of his eye, Vlad saw Jody and his new bride, Lacey, walking up to them.

Lacey linked her arm through Zoe's and asked where her date was.

"Funny thing, Lace. Vlad happened to walk over, said a couple of things, and off went my date. To take his dog out. What do you think of that?"

Lacey glared at Vlad. "Vlad, I adore you, you know I do, but one more time, and Jody won't be able to save you. Got it?" Lacey took Zoe's arm and led her over to the bar.

After putting a glass of wine in Zoe's hand, Lacey asked, "You want me to have Jody break his legs? Or maybe his jaw so he can't speak?"

Zoe smiled at her best friend. "You always have my back, don't you, Lace? Forget about Vlad. This is your wedding day!" Zoe took a look out over the beach at the different groups of people. Lacey and Jody had exactly the kind of wedding they wanted.

Even though the mothers of both bride and groom wanted a formal church wedding with all the fixings, Lacey and Jody got their way. They were married on the beach with only Vlad and Zoe standing up with them as best man and maid of honor. Lacey wore a simple, white lace dress, and Jody was wearing tan shorts and a pale green shirt. Lacey had a slight baby bump that she was enormously proud of, since doctors had told Jody years ago that he could never have children.

Zoe was watching a group of people playing volleyball, while others around them danced and shared laughs, mostly accompanied by drinks. "This really is the perfect wedding, Lace. Right up your alley. Mine, too. I've been to so many weddings, and none of them are as fun as this. What do you say we go take a dip in the ocean?"

"God, I would love to, but I really don't think that would be appropriate, would it? I mean, aren't I kind of supposed to be the hostess?" Jody overheard their conversation as he walked back up to them, thankfully without Vlad in tow.

He wrapped his arms around Lacey and stroked her belly. "Lace, if you want to go take a dip in the ocean, go do it." He pulled Zoe into his side, too. "I just want my girls to be happy today. Zoe, take my bride inside, put your suits on, and have a dip in the ocean." He let them go and smacked Lacey's bottom. "Have fun today, Angel, anyway you want to."

Lacey gave Jody a peck on the cheek and grabbed Zoe's hand. "Let's go swimming!" Then she turned and yelled a general invitation to her wedding guests. Before she knew it, about half a dozen people had run into the ocean, clothes and all.

Vlad watched all of it, wanting to join in the fun, but he was too distracted with thoughts of Zoe to be an active participant. More and more she was consuming his thoughts. He honestly didn't know what to do about her. Realistically, he knew he should give her up and move on. He'd even convinced himself he was ready to, but then, just like that, he saw some douchebag with her on his arm, and Vlad wanted to take him out. Take. Him. Out.

As he sat back and watched the people do what they would, he caught a glimpse of Zoe and Lacey—clad in bathing suits—coming back out of Jody's house. Lacey had on a simple, black one-piece, and Zoe had on typical Zoe attire.

She had a fantastic sense of style and liked to dress with flair. She would never wear something as simple as a black one-piece bathing suit. Nope, she had on a red—nothing bland for Zoe—string bikini. You know, the kind that was barely there? The kind that had actual strings hanging down from the skimpy bottoms and the even skimpier top? Yeah, that one.

Seriously? Christ. Vlad needed to stop the direction of his thoughts, or they were soon going to be blatantly obvious to anyone around him. *What time was this damn wedding over?* He needed to get the hell out of there. Pronto.

After another half hour of tormenting himself, he found Jody. "Hey, Chief. Great wedding. I'm really happy for you, man." Vlad pulled him in for a quick hug and gave him a slap on the back. "If you don't have anything else that you need me to take care of, I'm going to take off."

Vlad knew Jody saw him peeking at Zoe all night long. "Nah, I have everything I need. Thanks, though. You going to go home and drown your sorrows?" Jody asked, not masking the smirk that appeared on his face.

"Maybe." Vlad gave a smirk of his own. "Screw you man, you got the girl." He gave Jody one last slap on the back and turned to leave. As soon as he turned, he went down. "Goddammit!"

"Vlad! You okay? Have you had too much to drink? I'll drive you home, buddy."

Vlad looked up at Jody with pure rage on his face. "No. I have not had too much to drink. I just tripped, got it?"

"Okay, yeah, if you're sure." Vlad hadn't taken a drink other than the celebratory champagne all night. He gave him a hand, and Vlad limped toward his old car.

Chapter 2

Almost four weeks went by before Vlad saw Zoe again. Training Camp had started; therefore, mandatory therapy sessions had started as well. He was looking forward to seeing her, even though he was reasonably sure she wasn't feeling the same way.

Dalton "Cage" Booker, the backup goalie, was coming out of Zoe's house as Vlad pulled up. "Hey, Impaler, how's it hanging? Doc's looking smokin' today. Shame I can't tap that."

Vlad had been nicknamed "The Impaler" since, to his dismay, he shared his name with Vlad Dracula. He told anyone who asked, though, that it was because he had one of the best poke checks in the NHL.

Vlad gave Cage a jarring, *friendly* shove. "Don't talk about her like that, you little shit. She takes her job seriously. Show some respect for her position." Okay, maybe he was being a bit harsh, but Cage was one seriously annoying twenty-five year old kid. One of Cage's problems was that he was entirely too attractive, and he knew it.

Cage widened his eyes a bit at Vlad's reaction. "Dude, relax. Sorry, man. I should've known better since, well …"

Vlad crossed his arms and widened his stance. "Since, well, what? Care to elaborate?"

"Aw, come on, man. We all know you have it bad for the doc. I'm just saying I don't blame you. She's a hot little package. God, that ass, you know? Of course you know. Man, she bent over today, and all I could think about—"

Vlad grabbed Cage by his shirt, and pulled him close, just inches from his face. "Don't finish that sentence, unless you don't care about that pretty face of yours anymore." Still holding onto him, Vlad took a deep breath to calm himself. "Try not to be late for practice again, can ya, Booker?" He had to get away from that kid or he was going to do something he would possibly regret. Giving him one last menacing look, he pushed him away, hard enough to cause Cage to stumble and walked past him.

As Cage caught himself, he said, "Yeah, okay. Later."

Zoe was waiting at the door for him with half a smile on her face. "You don't have to defend me, you know. I can handle snot-nosed kids like Cage. Come on in."

Well, she's speaking to me. That's a good sign, he thought, as he followed her into the house and grabbed a beer from the fridge. Vlad felt at home in Zoe's house. He'd been there many times because of his relationship with Jody and Lacey. He could see how that would be difficult for most therapists, but Zoe maintained the two relationships separately with excellence.

"Help yourself to a beer, why don't you?" Waving her hand toward the back of the house, she added, "You know the way."

Vlad popped the lid off his beer bottle and walked back to the office. He plopped down in his typical seat and propped his legs up on the coffee table. At Zoe's raised eyebrows, he put them back down on the floor with a mumbled apology.

Zoe took her seat, grabbing her notebook on the way. "Okay, Vlad, let's talk. Tell me how you're feeling about starting the new season. Any issues you'd like to discuss? Do you have anything that you want to talk about before delving into the world of hockey for another season?"

"Nope."

"That's it? No worries after coming off a Stanley Cup win? That's all you have for today? I have to say, I'm not sure that's going to be enough for my notes to the coach." Zoe couldn't tell the coach exactly what they spoke about, but she did need to give him a brief summary of the session.

"You want me to make something up? My only issue is one that you're well aware of, and it's not on the table for discussion per *your* rules. But hey, you want me to talk? Fine. I need advice on how to get this awesome woman to give me a chance. See, here's the problem as I see it. She's not willing to try and figure out a way to be with me, even though I know she's crazy about me." Vlad gave her a smile. "Who could blame her? I'm a pretty terrific guy."

Zoe held her hand up. "Okay, stop. Vlad, please keep your personal feelings for me out of this. This is exactly why they don't let me date any players. I want— no—I *need* to be able to do my job."

Vlad stood up, knowing the session was a waste of time. Zoe would fill something in to appease the organization. "Fine. As usual, you're right. If I ever need to talk about anything, you'll be the first person I come to. I promise." He walked over to her, put his hands on her face, and placed a kiss on her forehead. Looking into her eyes for a second, he sighed and left.

After Vlad left, Zoe continued to stand in her office, processing the feeling of his lips on her skin. Any time he touched her, she got the shivers. Plus, she had to admit that it was rather nice to see him reaming Cage out for talking about her like she was a sex object.

She knew Vlad had hopes of them getting together again. Yes, again. Right before Lacey moved out to San Diego to live with her, she and Vlad had a remarkable night together. She remembered every detail. Even then she knew it was wrong, but one thing led to another, and the next thing she knew it was morning. She hadn't told another soul. Not even Lacey.

Vlad left Zoe's feeling like he often did around her. Frustrated. He was glad he had an afternoon practice. There was nothing like a good, sweaty workout to get his mind off his troubles. When he was in the net, he didn't have time to think of anything but stopping that six-ounce, frozen piece of rubber from getting past him.

Cage was in the locker room when Vlad walked in to get suited up. He made a quick exit to the rink, probably knowing Vlad still wanted to mop the floor with him. Vlad had always been a mentor to Cage, so he was sure it was obvious that he was less than pleased with the kid.

"Hey, Vlad, how's it going? Feeling good?" Keith Lambert was the Scorpions' captain and liked to make the rounds before practice. With over twenty guys in the room, it was easy for one person to get pissed at another—and people thought women were bad. Even though the coaches ran the practices, Keith wanted to know where their heads were. He wanted to know who was in the zone and who needed a little prodding to get their concentration on.

"Yeah, why? Did someone tell you I wasn't? Because it's not true, I'm fine." It seemed like lately everyone wanted to know how he was feeling. He didn't notice anyone else being grilled about how *they* were feeling all the time. His performance in the Stanley Cup finals last year was stellar. "There's nothing wrong with me. I had one of the best records last year, you know."

"Whoa, man. Where's all this coming from? I didn't mean I thought something was wrong with you; I'm just making my pre-practice rounds. I have to say, though, your reaction makes me wonder if there *is* something wrong. Anything you want to talk about?"

Vlad took a deep breath before answering Keith's questions. "Sorry, Keith. I guess I'm a little on edge today. I had a little disagreement with Cage, and I'm coming from the doc's. You know how much I love my therapy sessions. Don't worry, I'll get in the zone as soon as my blades hit the ice." He really had to

17

get a hold of himself. If he kept this up, people were going to get a little more than curious to find out if everything was as it should be with him.

Cage was too good of a goalie for Vlad to let his guard down. He could very easily lose his number one spot to that punk. He was man enough to admit that age played a factor in hockey.

Vlad strapped on his blue and silver goalie pads, grabbed his blocker and catching glove, and made his way to the ice. He passed Cage in the tunnel, speaking in low tones to Keith. He knew they were discussing him. "Everything okay here, boys?" Keith just nodded and led them out to the rink.

It was great to be back on the ice. The goals gleamed with their red posts and white netting. The lines and logo—a silver scorpion, tail curled in attack mode, clutching a hockey stick in its pinchers—had just been painted under the ice the previous week. It made a great tattoo, which Vlad had on his chest.

Skating over to his crease, Vlad took in the beauty of the freshly cleaned ice. It glistened, and he almost hated to ruin it. As he skated back and forth, shaving some of the ice off to make his crease a tad less slick, he could feel that ever present twitch in his hip. Hips and groin. Really important parts for a goalie to keep healthy, especially a butterfly goalie like him. Working through the pain was part of the job though, and after a couple of minutes, he no longer felt it.

Chapter 3

The first game of the season was upon them, and emotions were running high. It was a rival match between the San Diego Scorpions and the San Jose Sharks. Vlad had gotten the nod and was the starting goalie. As he skated onto the ice for warm ups, Cage wished him luck.

Vlad couldn't remember being as nervous as he was that night, and he wasn't quite sure why. He'd been the starting goalie in many season openers. His numbers from the prior season were phenomenal, and his body twinges weren't overly noticeable. What was his problem?

He didn't think it was because Jody wasn't there anymore. Jody had retired after they won the Cup in June so he would be around to help Lacey raise their baby. Even though Vlad missed having him near, he couldn't imagine that led to his uneasiness. Jody had been the team's enforcer and pretty much only played when they needed a physical presence on the ice, or to fill in for an injured player. Besides, Jody, Lacey, and Zoe were in the stands cheering the team on.

Vlad heard Brandon Marcoux, one of the Scorpions' young left-wingers, shout his name right before a puck hit him square in the chest. "Vlad, heads up, man!" Brandon skirted around the net and flipped another puck at him which went in on Vlad's glove side. "That's what happens to a butterfly goalie! Watch your glove side." He gave Vlad a wink and skated back to the red line to taunt the other team for a bit.

Vlad took a calming breath and squared himself in the net. Warm ups were coming to a close as he banged his stick side-to-side to feel where the posts were. He got in a half-bent stance and urged his teammates to give him all they had. They fired shots at him left and right. Brandon tried to sneak another one in on his glove side, directly above his left shoulder, but even though he had already started going down into the butterfly, at the last possible second, he committed a little left-handed larceny and stole the puck out of mid-air. Vlad gave him a shit-eating grin. "Ha! Fuck you, Marcoux! I still got it."

Brandon gave him a hearty laugh and a congratulatory slap of his stick on Vlad's pads. "Good man, take that attitude into the game, and they're toast!"

Vlad did indeed take that attitude into the game. At the end of the third period, the score was tied at one a piece with a minute left to go on the clock. The buzzer went off with the game still tied. No one scored in the five minute overtime either, so they were going to a shootout. It was one-on-one time—shooter versus goalie. Vlad loved shootouts. Shootouts were the reason he had one of the best poke check records in the league, but he had to remember that the shooters coming at him knew that.

The Sharks started with their best shooter. Johansson was a winger with a wicked shot. Vlad would not be going for a poke check on him. He couldn't go too far out of the net with that guy.

He also knew that Johansson usually shot high, and he focused on his body language. Vlad waited to see if he dropped his shoulder, usually indicating a high shot. As he got closer, there was no shoulder drop. *Shit, what's he doing?* Just as Vlad slammed his knees together to go down and protect his five-hole, he saw the shoulder drop. *Fucker!* He scrambled quickly to his feet, but missed the puck as it sailed in high over his right shoulder.

The Scorpions' first shooter was their captain. Keith didn't waste any time with fancy skating. Grabbing the puck from the red center line, he charged ahead and went head on with Price to try and sneak the puck in low just past his right pad. It looked like a perfect shot until the puck hit his pad and bounced out in front of him, never crossing the goal line. Keith skated back to the bench, banging his stick in frustration as he left the ice.

The next shooter was the Sharks' captain, Tommy Xavier. Vlad hadn't faced him before in a shootout and wasn't sure exactly what to expect. Xavier took his time and skated the puck back and forth before taking his shot. He went high and the puck, once again, sailed in over Vlad's right shoulder. *Goddammit!*

Next up was Spicer, a fairly new guy to the Scorpions with mad puck handling skills. When he tried to finesse his puck into Price's net, and Price blocked the shot, things really got desperate.

Since Vlad had let the first two pucks in and the Sharks had denied the Scorpions' first two shots, the next puck had to go in. Marcoux was up for the Scorpions. If he missed, it was over. His shot went high, hitting the post, and that was that. The Sharks had won in a shootout.

The team was understandably subdued as the players filed back into the locker room. Vlad pushed off his net to follow them and went down on the ice. He quickly looked around and got back up, but it wasn't easy. His hip was becoming more of a problem. He didn't want the team to suffer for any of his inadequacies, but he wasn't ready to tell the team doctor about what he'd found out. He wasn't even supposed to have been seen by any other doctors, so he was hoping to never have to say anything.

Back in the locker room, Coach DeLeon was addressing the team. "You guys showed a great effort out there. I'm not going to point out the things that went wrong. It was the first game, and you know what went wrong. Practice is at nine tomorrow morning. Be ready to sweat." With a sadistic smile, the coach walked out.

Keith clapped his hands to get the room's attention. "Okay. We all know what that smile means. Tomorrow's practice is gonna suck." Keith laughed. "We looked okay out there, but we have better in us, don't we?" When all he got was some half-hearted, mumbled acquiescence, he threw his glove at a locker. "Don't be careless just because it was the first game, guys. Don't do that! We have more to give, and we'll give it!" Keith got the response he wanted from that and left the room.

"Gotta admit, Lambert can get his point across, can't he?" Looking at Vlad, Cage continued, "Hey old man, you feelin' okay? I saw you take a spill on your way off the ice. Need some Ben Gay? I'm ready to fill in at anytime."

"Booker, you really need to learn to keep your trap shut. Bring your attitude to practice and earn my spot. Until then, fuck off." Vlad was seriously getting tired of listening to Cage's ramblings. The guys teased each other all the time, and Vlad could take it as well as he could dish it out, but with Cage, he had a hard time letting it go. If he were being honest with himself, he could admit that it might be because Cage was hitting too close to home.

A couple of days later, Vlad was sitting on his patio watching the sun set. Seeing the bright red, yellow and orange streaks the sun left in the sky reminded him of how inconsequential his problems were in the grand scheme of things. He knew he should man up and talk to someone about what he'd been going through. It was time. His head knew it. The problem was that his heart and his pride were a bit slow to catch up.

He hadn't talked to Jody for a couple of days, so he gave him a call.

"Hey Vlad, how's it goin?"

"All right."

Vlad knew from Jody's pause that he wasn't buying it. Jody tried again. "So, what's up? You okay?"

There it was again. The *you okay?*.

"Yeah. Just checking in with you, is that a problem now too?" He just wanted to shoot the shit with someone without them asking if he was okay. Was that too much to ask?

"No, of course not. Should it be? Forget it. How was practice?"

Vlad sighed. "It was okay. To tell you the truth Chief, that Cage kid is killing me. I want to ring his oh-so-perfect neck. Christ! He just doesn't let up, you know?"

"Yeah, I do know. I don't care for the kid much myself, but you gotta let it slide off your back."

"He's just trying to get me to fuck up so he can take my place, I know it. That little prick will do anything to be the starting goalie. Well, screw him; I'm not going to just hand it over to him."

"No one's asking you to, Vlad. I agree that he's a little prick, but we all were at that age. I don't think he's trying to cheat you out of your spot. I think he'd rather earn it honestly. I think his mouth just gets away from him. I couldn't tell you how many times he's called me old or ancient or decrepit. He's just cocky."

Vlad would probably have agreed with Jody if he wasn't currently battling his own demons, but he was in a piss-poor mood lately and hated everyone. "He's not just cocky. I'm telling you man, he's gunning for me, and he's gonna get a stick up his ass if he doesn't back off."

Vlad was so angry. So much for his peaceful sunset. His behavior was far from his norm. Vlad was the guy everyone wanted to be around. He didn't get mad. Girls loved him, guys wanted to be him. Nothing was ever too much for him to handle.

"It sounds like you had a shit day, Vlad. How about we go out and grab a couple of beers? It's not too late and Lacey's not feeling so well tonight. The baby keeps kicking her in the bladder, and she wants me off her back. Seriously man, I try to help and she tells me to leave her alone. I feel helpless."

Vlad finally gave up a laugh. "Yeah, okay. But give her some slack, man. She's the best thing that ever happened to you. Don't fuck it up." Vlad was certainly happy for Jody, but that didn't mean he wasn't jealous. He'd do anything to have his girl demanding that he leave her alone because she was pregnant with his kid. Well, at least he had the part down where she demanded he leave her alone.

When Vlad and Jody got to the pub, they settled at the bar with a couple of beers.

"You guys want something to eat tonight?" Dan, the bartender, was used to having the NHLers in his place. He even had a private room in the back he let them use if the public attention got to be too much.

"I'm starving, Dan. Got any specials today?" Vlad was always starving. He was lucky he had a great metabolism. The way he ate, he should be as big as a house.

"Tony made up some of that crab bisque that everyone loves just this afternoon. He also made some cheddar biscuits. Want to start with that?"

"Yeah, that sounds great. How about you?" Vlad turned to see if Jody wanted the soup and spotted Zoe walking in. "Crap." He rubbed the back of his neck in agitation.

"What?" Jody turned in the direction Vlad was looking to see her walking right toward them. "Hey Zoe, you want to have a seat? Lace isn't here. Our little angel is into sparring mode again, and she's sick of me at the moment."

Zoe smiled, and put her arm around him in a show of support. She really did feel bad for Jody. He tried to do everything for Lacey, and it was driving her nuts. Zoe patted his cheek with true affection. "No thank you, sweets. I'm actually here to pick up some of that crab bisque for Lacey."

"What? No way! I asked her if she wanted anything before I left." He looked so forlorn. "I just want to help her."

Zoe explained for what seemed like the thousandth time. "Jody. Honey. Listen to me. She loves you more than chocolate, remember? She does, but you're just a bit, well, smothering. She needs some girl time, okay?"

"Okay, but make sure you get extra cheddar biscuits. She loves them."

"Oh, you poor deluded man. She *used* to love them. She hates cheddar cheese now. You bring them in the house and she'll puke all over you. As a matter of fact, you may not even want to eat them. She'll smell them on you." Zoe thought Lacey was a bit on the crazy side, too, but who was she to say? She'd never been pregnant.

Vlad smiled at Zoe. He honestly couldn't help it. Seeing how much she cared about Lacey warmed his heart. Zoe was such an amazing human being. She was loving, but crass and sarcastic. She was perfect. Okay, maybe she wasn't perfect, but she was to him. "Hey Zoe, you look especially pretty tonight." *Shut up, shut up, shut up,* Vlad told himself. *Go back to being agitated.*

Zoe looked down at her ripped jeans, red tank top, and half a dozen bangle bracelets. "Yeah, I guess I do, thanks."

"And so humble. What a great combination."

"Life's too short to be humble. I know I look good, but I don't flaunt it." Zoe smiled, but then looked away. "Well, I have to get this soup and run. I'm spending a bit of time with Lacey before I go on my date." As soon as the words were out of her mouth, she knew she made a mistake.

Vlad's hand clenched his beer bottle. "Really. A date, huh? Who's the lucky guy this time? Tim? Kyle? Steve? John? Pete?"

Jody cut him off. "Vlad, don't do that, man. You know Zoe's like a sister to me. Don't disrespect her." Zoe knew Vlad was putting Jody in a tough spot over whose side to take. That wasn't fair of him.

Zoe patted Jody on the back. "Thanks Jody, but it's okay. I understand him. He can't accept a situation that's beyond his control so he lashes out with insults. It's a coping mechanism." *Take that, Vlad.* "Since you asked, I'm going out with Sebastian. You know, that hot Spanish guy I met at that speed dating thing?" Why was she egging him on? She was as bad as he was sometimes.

That did it. Vlad was furious now. "You have got to be fucking kidding me! Jody told me you didn't have any 'sparks' with that guy. Shit, I can't do this anymore. Maybe I'll ask for a trade." Vlad got up and started walking out of the bar. Zoe followed after him, cheeks burning in shame.

"Vlad, wait." She grabbed his arm and turned him around. "I'm sorry. That was very insensitive of me, but you had it coming after that comment. You know the deal. We've been over and over this. We can't be together. Sebastian's a nice guy, and I enjoy his company. I don't know if anything will come of our dating, but I'm willing to try. I'm sick of being alone." Dropping her voice to a tone not much above a whisper, she said, "We can't keep having this same discussion, Vlad. We just can't." Zoe had tears in her eyes when she looked up at him. Zoe *never* cried. Never.

"Okay, Zoe. You win. Yet again, I'm sorry. Have a great date." Vlad walked back into the bar just as Jody was walking out. Jody handed Zoe the soup she came for and walked back in with Vlad.

"Sorry about that. I know I need to get it together around her. I'm really going to try. There's been this girl that comes to practice all the time. She might be a puck bunny, but she seems better than that. Maybe I'll ask her out and see how it goes. She's given me her number a dozen times. I have it in my locker. What do you think?"

Dating the puck bunnies was a mistake, but like he said, maybe this girl was different.

"I think it's a start. Going on a date is a good way to get moving in the right direction anyway. Go for it."

Chapter 4

Zoe's date with Sebastian was just like all the others, kind of flat. It wasn't that she didn't have a good time, because she did. The problem was that he wasn't Vlad. She had dated Sebastian a couple of times before, and they both agreed there was just no chemistry between them. Then they met up at the grocery store, of all places, and decided to try again. Still no spark.

When they left the restaurant, Sebastian took the opportunity to kiss her before they got into the car. He laughed, probably at Zoe's expression when he pulled back from her lips. "I think it says a lot that I'm not even insulted by that look on your face. I feel like I just inappropriately kissed my sister. Let's not try dating anymore and move onto friendship. What do you say?"

Zoe released a breath and let out a relieved laugh. "I think that's the best idea you've had tonight. What were we thinking anyway? Our first time dating wasn't much different." She put her arm around Sebastian's waist and gave him a squeeze.

"Since we got that out of the way, what do you say we go back to your house and take a stroll on the beach?"

Zoe smiled her first sincere smile of the night. "Sounds like a plan. If it's still light enough, want to throw the Frisbee around or something?"

"You're on. I know you like to compete, so how about whoever misses it the most pays for ice cream at that place near your house?" Zoe loved the idea. And it was even better when he lost and had to buy.

They walked the six blocks to the ice cream shop from Zoe's house. As soon as they entered, the hostess seated them, handing them menus. When the waitress walked over with glasses of water, Zoe reached out to take hers the same moment she saw Vlad walk in the door, with whom she assumed was his date. The glass slipped out of her hand and hit the table with a thud. It didn't break, but it made a hell of a noise and water went flying.

Sebastian grabbed the glass and glanced over to see what had startled her. She looked at him and was horrified to see that his shirt was soaked.

"Shit! I'm sorry." How embarrassing!

"Hey, it's just a little water, no big deal."

She sighed and shook her head. "Vlad just walked in. With a date. Do you mind if we leave?"

"I don't mind, Zoe, but I think we should stay. I realize I only know a little bit about your thing with him, but maybe it's good for both of you to get used to seeing each other with other people. But that's just my two cents. You want to leave? Just say the word."

Dammit, why couldn't she have feelings for this guy? He was nice and considerate. He had a good job, a healthy relationship with his family, and was quite the hottie. It made no logical sense that they felt nothing for each other beyond friendship. "No. You're right. Let's just order our ice cream, eat the damn stuff, and get it over with."

"Wow. You're a dream date, you know that? I'll try not to let your love for me go to my head." Sebastian gave her a wink so she knew he was only playing with her.

"You know what, Sebastian? I think you and I are going to be great friends." She got a sneaky look in her eyes and continued, "You know, there's this girl in the marketing department that I think would be perfect for you. She's got a five year old little girl, though. What do you think?"

"I think I'd love to meet her. I trust your opinion, and I'm not afraid of a woman with a child. I like kids. Aside from that, I'm tired of being alone. You know, I don't get it. I think I'm a nice guy, I have a steady income, I'm not totally ugly, and I treat a lady like a lady. Why the hell am I still single?" Sebastian looked so completely baffled; Zoe had to laugh at him.

"Who knows? Look how friggin' adorable I am, and I'm still single. Sometimes the world is just a bit off kilter."

"Yeah, but your situation is different. You've already found your love. You just haven't figured out how to make it work yet."

Vlad could not believe Zoe and that Spanish dude were there. What were the chances? Okay, well the chances really weren't that unlikely. The ice cream shop was only five or six blocks from Zoe's place. It made him wonder if, subconsciously, he was hoping she might be there. Jesus, now he sounded like her when she did her psychoanalysis bullshit on him. Although, much to his chagrin, she was usually right.

"Vlad? Did you hear me, baby?" He hated that Cindy was already using pet names. It was their first date! And what a mistake it was.

"No, sorry. Huh?"

"I asked if you wanted to come home with me. You don't have to wonder why. I'm a sure thing, baby." She slid her leg up his thigh under the table as she licked her lips. When he moved his legs, she got angry with him. "All right, what's the deal? I thought you'd want to have sex with me."

Well, she certainly was straight forward. "Look Cindy, I think this was a mistake. I thought you were one of the nice girls who maybe wanted to get to know me. Let me just take you home."

It was clear Cindy didn't like that response as she picked up her water glass and dumped it on him. "I'll get my own ride home. I can't believe I wasted an entire night on you. My friends were right: I should have gone with one of the younger guys."

"Yeah, whatever. See ya." Trying in vain to mop up the water on his shirt with the two tiny napkins on the table, Vlad figured he got what he deserved. The only time he should go out with a puck bunny was when he just wanted some tail. He got up and walked over to Zoe's table.

"Hey Doc, Jose."

Zoe saw red. "His name is Sebastian, Vlad, as you well know. What happened to your date? Does she have school tomorrow? Had to meet curfew?" Shit! Why was she baiting him again?

Vlad laughed off her comment. "Funny stuff, Zoe. But no, we just weren't meant to be. Some people are meant to be together and some aren't. You know what I mean, don't you?" He tugged on her blouse. "Like Jody and Lacey."

Sebastian appeared amused at their interaction. He had mentioned earlier that he thought Vlad and Zoe had fire between them, whatever that meant. Zoe was pretty sure he had some special power to see what people were feeling beneath the façade they showed to the world. He was definitely an interesting guy. She thought again that it really was shame she only thought of him as a friend.

"Yes, actually I do know what you mean. Those two *were* meant to be together, but some people aren't. However, I do understand that not everyone is smart enough to realize when they're fighting a losing battle. You know what *I* mean, don't you, Vlad?" Zoe crossed her arms and raised an eyebrow.

"Sure. But you have to admit—sometimes the smarter ones are the ones who lose out. Life is all about taking chances. *Sometimes* you even have to interfere to get what you want.

What's the point in playing it safe if there's something so incredible right in front of you?" He looked at her with a tenderness that was hard for her to process. "So extraordinarily incredible." Vlad tugged on her blouse once more and left.

"That was entertaining. You two are a mess. Come on, Zoe. Let's get our ice cream to go. We can go sit on your deck and talk for a while. Sound good?"

Zoe thought that was a great idea. She could use someone to talk to, and she knew Lacey would be asleep by now. "You really are going to be a great friend, aren't you? I feel so comfortable around you, and ask anyone, that's rare. I don't trust so easily. Of course I'm usually the happy-go-lucky kind of girl. Vlad just pushes all my buttons."

"You might be better off if you actually did let him push your buttons."

"Oh, I see what you're doing. Real nice. Okay … well, for you information, we've been there, done that."

She could see that *that* shocked him. "You slept with your client? You've got to be kidding me. Oh, this just got so much more interesting."

"I'm trusting you to keep your mouth shut. What is it about you that makes me spill my guts?" Zoe still hadn't even told Lacey yet. Their whole conversation was crazy, even for her.

Sebastian looked her in the eye and reassured her. "I would never tell a soul what you told me in confidence. I know we don't know each other very well, but I feel a strong connection to you. I'm sure you think it's all voodoo crap or some other kind of psychic BS, but it's not. There's a reason we were put together.

We know that we don't have a romantic connection, but maybe I'm here to help you. Or just listen. Whatever it is, I'm here."

Zoe let out a relieved sigh. "Okay. I guess I could use someone to talk to. I hate to burden Lacey with my drama right now. The baby's been keeping her up at night lately, and she's not getting much sleep."

"The baby? Isn't she still pregnant?"

"Oh yeah, she is. I mean the baby's been sitting on her bladder a lot and has recently started kicking her at all hours of the night. I hate to give her more to think about or worry over right now, you know?"

"Sure. So let's get our ice cream and vamoose."

Chapter 5

It was almost three weeks until the Halloween game, and Zoe was in Lacey's living room discussing their costumes. A lot of people dressed up for the game, and it was fun to take part in. There was even a contest for the best costume. The previous year, Zoe dressed as a belly dancer, and Lacey was a fallen angel.

"You should be the fallen angel again. That would be a sight. A pregnant angel would definitely be fallen." Zoe was going to dress in something sexy as usual.

"Hey," Lacey said, swinging the subject back to Zoe. "Why don't you go as Elvira?"

"Have you actually *seen* Elvira? Her boobs are huge." Zoe cupped herself. "Look at these girls, Lace. Look at them! They're tiny. Ain't no way I could pull off Elvira."

"Hmmm, well I guess you have a point. How about a devil? That suits you better anyway."

"Bite me, Lace. Devils have been done to death. Besides, I want to dress ultra sexy this year. I need something that's going to attract some men. I want to start dating again."

"Really? Dating, as in, seeing someone you might actually have chemistry with?" When Zoe told her that she and Sebastian had decided to just be friends, Lacey wasn't surprised at all. She told Zoe that she thought the only reason she even agreed to go out with him again was because she already *knew* there was no chemistry between them—he was safe.

Zoe looked up at the ceiling. "Yes, Lacey. You're right. I need to step out of my comfort zone and really give dating a chance. I don't want to be alone, you know."

"I know, but I don't see the Vlad situation changing anytime soon. There's no reason you shouldn't be enjoying a guy or two."

"I think those days are long gone. I'm not looking for a casual fling. I'm tired of being the one night girl, you know?"

"Jeez, Zoe. You make yourself sound like a tramp. There's nothing wrong with having a couple of casual relationships every year if that's what you want to do."

"That's the thing, Lace. I don't think that is all I want anymore. I'm just not sure how to move forward when Vlad's always around. It seems like everywhere I look, there he is."

Jody walked in then with yet another bouquet of flowers. "Hi, girls. Don't mind me." He handed Lacey the flowers, kissed her on the cheek and started to walk out of the room.

"You don't have to go, Jody. I have to head out anyway. I have an appointment in about an hour." Keith Lambert had actually made a voluntary appointment with her. She hoped everything was okay with the captain. She'd soon find out.

Keith showed up right on schedule. Zoe led him back to her office, and they got down to business.

"I'm here about Vlad." Before Zoe could stop him, he put up his hand. "Wait. It's not about the two of you. I'm worried about him. Something's not right. You know Vlad. He's the happy guy—the guy that's always easy to talk to, and fun to be around, but lately he's been a total ass. It's like his personality has totally changed. There has to be a reason. I don't know what to do with him, and it's starting to affect my locker room. I can't have that."

Zoe sat there chewing on her pen. "Keith, you know I try my best to help everyone who walks through my door, but I can't help Vlad if he won't talk to me. This whole situation is getting out of control. I'm going to have to go to management. If Vlad is really having a problem, and he won't talk to me, he's going to have to go talk to someone else."

That was Zoe's greatest fear. She'd have to talk to management and hope they didn't let her go. It was the exact situation she'd been trying to avoid. But the players had to come first. Logically, she understood that, but shit, she was mad. She told Vlad no. She did the right thing, and he still might cause her to lose her job. *Dammit!*

"No, Zoe. Don't go to management yet. Maybe we can tag team him. Better yet, maybe you and Jody could do that. He probably won't open up with me here. Even though it's blatantly obvious to everyone, including management, by the way, that you two have a, shall we say, *connection*, I don't think you should inform them that there's a problem there. That's not fair to you."

"The idea has merit. At this point, what do we have to lose? I'll talk to Jody and see what he thinks. Do you have any ideas what his problem could be?"

Keith thought about that for a minute. Gesturing toward her he said, "Aside from the obvious, I can't think of much. I know that Cage annoys the hell out of him, but Cage annoys the hell out of everyone. He's been riding Vlad pretty hard lately with the snarky comments. All age related, of course. Cocky little shit. I'm honestly afraid that Vlad might physically hurt Cage, and that's not Vlad, you know? Normally, he would give Cage a taste of his own medicine, or just turn the other cheek. He's really changed."

"Okay. Since this is more of a friendly visit, and not a session, I'll be honest with you. I've obviously noticed the difference, too. Not to toot my own horn or anything, but I think a lot of it has to do with me. You should have heard how he talked to me when he found out I had a date. He was downright nasty. Vlad has never been anything but flirty and nice to me. What we need to figure out is if it is *just* me or if there is something else going on."

"Yeah, I know. It's frustrating. I don't know what do with him, but I can't let his attitude infect the rest of the team. If I let that negativity fester in the locker room, it will begin to affect the other players. I'm at a loss. Coach doesn't like his attitude any more than I do."

"Have you talked to him?"

"Yeah, but he doesn't listen. He just gets pissed and tells me everything is okay, which it obviously is not."

"All right, Keith. I'll talk to Jody and see what he thinks. He's the closest to him, so hopefully he'll be able to help."

Keith got up to leave. "Thanks. What do you say we don't document this visit? I want to help Vlad, not stir up a shit storm, you know?"

"Absolutely. You're a great captain, you know that? I knew they made the right choice when they made you captain."

Keith stood a little taller at her praise. "Thank you. That means a lot to me. This team is everything. They're my family, you know?"

"Yes. I see how you all are. I think it's cute."

"Cute? Christ girl, I'm a man. It's not cute. It's, well, more like—maybe sweet is a better word? Yeah, not really. Shit, I need to go shoot some pool now or maybe go lift some heavy things for a while." Keith winked at her and let himself out.

Chapter 6

Zoe called Jody to talk about Vlad. Lacey answered the phone, and Zoe could tell she was in one of her pouty moods. She loved Lacey more than almost anyone in her life, but she would be happy as hell when she was back to her normal, self-sufficient, confident self.

Sounding pissed off, Lacey asked Zoe why she wanted to talk to Jody.

"I wanted to talk to him about Vlad." Taking a deep breath, Zoe continued, "What's wrong, Lace?"

"Nothing. Jody is perfect. He made a really nice dinner, although since he can't cook for shit, it sucks. I wanted pasta alfredo with zucchini and black olives. Addie is all over me tonight, and I just want to eat!"

In her most smoothing voice, Zoe said, "Okay, how about this? I'll come make that for you. I actually have a batch of alfredo sauce that I made a couple of weeks ago in the freezer. I'll thaw that out and stop at the store to buy some great veggies. What kind of pasta do you want, hun?" Zoe didn't mind cooking for her. She liked that she could make Lacey feel better.

"Zoe, you are the best. How about fettuccine? And can you add hot chili peppers in there, too?" A strange combination, but what the baby wanted, the baby got. "And maybe some Rocky Road ice cream? With crème de mint sauce?"

Zoe held back a gag. "Anything you want. Don't be offended when you see that I've made me and Jody something a bit tamer, okay?"

Lacey finally gave her a laugh. "That's fine. I know my eating habits are pretty strange these days. Thanks, Zoe. See you soon."

Zoe and Jody talked while she cooked in Lacey's kitchen.

"So what do you think about Keith's idea? Do you think it might work if you and I tag team him, or do you think it'll just piss him off?"

"I'm not sure, but I think we have to give it a shot. He seems to be getting worse and worse. How much damage could we do? But I think you're the one he's going to go after." Jody walked over to her and gave her a squeeze. "I think you need to wear your thickest skin. You know how much he loves you. He only speaks to you like that out of hurt and frustration."

"I know. Would you believe I've actually thought about leaving the organization? This thing between Vlad and me isn't healthy for anyone. But I don't see a solution, do you?"

"Well, it is the last year of Vlad's contract. No one knows where he'll be next year."

"I don't even want to think about that. Not seeing him would be even worse than this fucked up thing we have going. Jesus, I need my *own* therapist. I know better, but it's hard to make your heart listen, you know?" Zoe wasn't stupid. She knew that some of the things she told her clients were next to impossible to follow through with. She still believed she told them the right things; she just had a better perspective now on how hard it was to *do* the right thing.

"Well, I don't know exactly what you guys are going through, but I remember Lace telling me that she didn't want a relationship in the beginning. She only wanted to casually date. I wanted her to change her mind so bad that I lost sleep over it. I'd lie awake at night and think of things that I could do to weasel my way into her heart. I got lucky. I mean, this pregnancy aside, she's damn near perfect. I really don't deserve her."

Zoe knew how much Jody loved Lacey. And she knew he was ecstatic that Lacey was pregnant. "Awww, Jody. Yes, you do. And you know I don't say that lightly. Lacey is closer to me than even a sister could be. You do deserve her."

Jody smiled. "Thanks." Looking over her ingredients for dinner, his smile vanished. "Zoe? Do you think Lace would freak if I ordered a pizza?"

Zoe laughed and shook her spoon at him. "Jody LaGrange! Do you really think *we're* eating this crap? I already told Lacey that you and I were not eating her weird shit. We're safe. We're having simple shrimp alfredo. Does that work for you?"

"Zoe, I love you." He kissed her head and went into the living room to check on Lacey and set the table for dinner.

"I can't wait to eat. It smells awesome in there. How are you feeling, Lace?"

"Good today. I'm hungry though, as usual." She pushed herself up off the couch. "I'm going to see if I can help Zoe. I'm tired of sitting here."

"Okay. I'll set the table."

Dinner tasted as good as it smelled. Talking with a mouth full of the bread, Lacey said, "Oh my God, Zoe. This is the absolute freaking best garlic bread you've ever made. Addie hasn't kicked me since I started eating!" They all laughed at that.

"Good thing we're not having twins, huh, Angel? You'd be as big as a house with the way you need to eat now." Zoe kicked him. Hard. Was he insane making remarks like that?

Lacey looked at him with eyes wide and full of tears.

"Fuck! No! Lace, baby, that's not what I meant. I meant, crap, I don't know what I meant. I want you to be as big as a house—I mean you're so beautiful. If you were having twins, you'd be twice as beautiful, if that were even possible. I love to watch you eat. I think it's endearing. You eat to nourish our baby. You have no idea how much I appreciate how you care for her." Lacey was full of curves. Zoe knew that Jody loved those curves. He'd never want her to be like those skinny models, but he couldn't seem to stop rambling and back-tracking, and Zoe couldn't help but hold back a smirk at poor Jody's foot-in-mouth issues.

Lacey, more like her pre-pregnancy self, full of piss and vinegar, said, "If I were having twins, you wouldn't even be eating right now, because there wouldn't be enough! Now, pass me some more garlic bread and let me eat in peace."

Zoe looked at poor Jody and changed the subject from food to Vlad. "Okay." Giving Lacey a pointed look, she continued, "Now that we've all had enough to eat, let's figure out what the hell we're going to do about Vlad."

She filled Lacey in on her meeting with Keith. Lacey wasn't as concerned about tiptoeing around Vlad. "You guys just need to go over there and talk to him. Enough is enough. He's being ridiculous now. Lashing out at teammates, being rude to Zoe. Enough. After you two are done eating, go right over there. I'm feeling pretty good tonight; Addie must've loved dinner, too. I'll do dishes, you two go tackle Vlad." Lacey got up and cleared their plates. She gave Zoe a kiss on the cheek. "Thank you so much for dinner. It was exactly what I needed. And I can't wait for the ice cream and mint sauce!"

"Wow, Lace. Ick." Zoe smiled at her. "I'm glad you enjoyed it. We'll let you know what happens with Vlad. Wish us luck. I think we're going to need it."

Vlad was playing NHL 13, featuring Philadelphia's Claude Giroux on the cover. He admired the hell out of that kid and was glad he didn't have to face him much during the season. When the doorbell rang, he looked at the clock noticing that it was almost eight. *God, don't let it be that puck bunny.* He didn't think she would know where he lived, but one never knew what personal information a nosey body could find.

He wasn't as relieved as he should have been when he looked out the peep hole to see Jody and Zoe standing there. *Great, an intervention?* Even though he had misgivings, he opened the door. Zoe *was* out there, after all.

He wasn't sure if he succeeded, but he went for a casual air. "Hey. What are you guys doing here?" *Yeah, that didn't sound too inviting.*

Zoe lifted an eyebrow at him. "We're fine, thanks. Why yes, we'd love to come in. Thank you ever so much." She pushed past him and entered the place she'd only been in once before. When she looked at the coffee table, she blushed.

"Bring back fond memories, does it?"

"Vlad!"

Vlad decided to play nice and asked them if they wanted something to drink. "Hell, yes. Lacey can't stand the smell of beer anymore, and I could definitely use a Molson. Please tell me you have some."

Zoe wanted something stronger. It was harder than she thought it would be to be back in his condo. What a fantastic night they had. And what a terrible mistake it'd been. "I'd love some scotch if you have it."

"You know I do, Zoe. If I remember correctly, the last time you were here ..."

"Stop, Vlad. Please." Turning to Jody, she said, "I shouldn't have come. This was a mistake."

Vlad knew he was being an ass—again. What was his problem? Zoe didn't do anything to him other than maintain her professionalism so she could keep her job. He should admire that, so why was he being such an asshole? He truly didn't know. Maybe he just wanted her to hurt because he was hurting.

He wrapped his hand around his neck, rubbing and squeezing. "No, Zoe, don't go. I'm sorry. I don't know what my problem is, but it's not you." Maintaining eye contact, he continued, "I can't help where my thoughts wander where you're concerned. Yes, I know that's not allowed, yadda, yadda, and so on ..." Just looking at her made his heart thunder in his chest. He cleared his throat and looked over at Jody. "So, I assume this isn't just a friendly visit. What's up?"

Jody started talking. "Well, we're all a bit concerned about you, man. Before you get pissed off, let me explain. Maybe you don't see it, but you used to be the happy, laid back guy who everyone wanted to be around, but lately, you're ... well, honestly, you've been acting like an asshole. You lash out at your teammates and the girl you love." Jody looked at Zoe, mumbling, "Sorry, but it's true."

"Oh, come on, what the fuck is this? You get the two people I'm closest to and play 'What's wrong with Vlad?' Maybe I'm just sick of things lately. Maybe I'm just struggling with being an older goalie, or Cage gunning for my spot, or watching *my girl* go out on dates." At that last part, he looked to Zoe. "Come on Zoe,

47

you're the shrink. Do you think that might be enough to piss a guy off now and then? What do you say?" Vlad threw the whiskey glass he was holding into the fireplace, making Zoe flinch at the sound of the exploding glass.

"Come on, Vlad. Talk to me." Zoe tried to avoid, at all costs, talking to Vlad about her feelings. "You know how I feel about you. You know why it can't be, but that doesn't lessen my feelings. Talk to me."

Zoe was grateful that Jody took that as his cue to step into the other room.

"Goddammit, Zoe. It's not that easy. You just don't get it. There is no one else in the entire world like you. No one will ever compare to you. Fuck! I just—I don't know how to say it. I *have* to have you. I just have to." He shook his head in defeat. He couldn't stop himself if his life depended on it. He marched over to her, grabbed her on either side of her face and pressed his lips to hers. It wasn't a sweet kiss, or even a passionate one. It was punishing. Desperate. He didn't know what to do with his emotions so he poured them into his kiss.

Feeling emotionally drained herself, she pushed him away. It wasn't easy to do. Fighting their attraction became harder each day, and she had no idea what to do about it. Keeping her voice at a whisper she said, "Vlad, I'm sorry I keep pushing you away. I just don't know what else to do." She threw her hands up and started pacing in front of him. "I know there's something else going on with you. Your personality has changed so much in the past six months. If you can't talk to me, you have to find someone you can talk to." Staring down at her clenched hands, she said, "I'm really worried about you. Please, Vlad, you need to talk to someone. This isn't only about us. Your attitude is affecting your team."

Zoe left Vlad standing there, shaking his head. "Great. Go ahead and leave, Zoe, but know this. I'm done trying to figure this out. I want you, and I'll have you. Go ahead and try to date. I'll interfere with every goddamn one. You understand? You're mine, Zoe Millis, and I'm going to prove it to you. I'm going to ruin you for all other men." Okay, that sounded a bit creepy, borderline stalkerish, but he knew she got the point.

She looked at him with her shoulders hung in defeat. "That's the problem, Vlad. I think you already have." She grabbed Jody and walked out the door.

Chapter 7

Over the following weeks, Zoe dated. She said yes to every guy who asked her out. Normally, she simply ignored them or politely turned them away. Now, though, she was on a mission. For her own sanity, she needed to find a guy who could compete with Vlad for her affections. And really, just distract her from herself. She didn't want to think of Vlad in that way. There was no point. But at the same time, she couldn't seem to stop.

Her first date was pretty much what she expected, with a bit of a twist to the end.

She'd met Johnny in the bowling alley when she was there with a crew from work. He was there with his own friends in the lane next to hers. They got to talking and set plans up to have dinner the following night.

Johnny picked her up at seven o'clock, and they went to the local pizza joint, in Zoe's attempt to keep things casual.

"I've actually never been here. Have you?" Johnny was somewhat new to San Diego.

Zoe had been there plenty of times. "Yeah. They have great pizza. What do you like on yours?"

That was the first strike. "Anchovies and garlic. Then, when it comes to the table piping hot, you smother it with the dried red peppers."

Zoe smiled in good humor, teasing him, but she would never eat that crap!

"Fine, you buy what you want, and I'll buy what I want," Johnny retorted.

Cool first date, dude. So much for being a gentleman. "Okay, great." Since she'd never eat a whole pizza by herself, she ordered chicken tenders and fries.

Halfway through dinner, she was ready to call it quits. To make it even worse, Vlad walked in. *Oh, hell no. Not again.*

She quickly grabbed Johnny's hand and smiled up at him.

"What's that smile for?" He looked totally dumbfounded, which was not going to help her cause.

"Because I'm enjoying myself. You're good company." He seemed appeased and started rubbing her hand. She hated it, but Vlad was looking right at them.

"I'm glad, Zoe. I think we could be good together."

Really, you freak? Who the fuck are you kidding? They had nothing in common. Basically, he was an idiot and she wasn't.

"You think we'll fuck tonight?"

Holy shit! He did not just say that. Zoe was far, far away from being a prude, but come on! Was this guy for real? But what could she do? Vlad had just taken a seat next to them. She knew he was listening to everything they said.

"I think that's a very good possibility." She hated herself for even saying it. Hated herself more when she heard a water glass breaking on the floor directly behind her. At least she knew

Vlad was aware of her, right? Ugh. Granted, she shouldn't be torturing him when *she* was the one who kept denying *him*. She thought, once again, that *she* was the one who needed therapy.

"Let's blow this joint so you can blow something else, baby. What do you say?"

Before Zoe could formulate an answer, Vlad was there. Legs planted wide apart, arms crossed, he bellowed, "Zoe Millis! Mother is worried sick! You didn't take any of your medications. What are we supposed to do when you leave the house like that?" Vlad then addressed her date. "I'm really sorry about this, man. She got out on us. We're usually good about controlling her, but when she takes on this personality, she gets sneaky."

Zoe started sputtering at Vlad. How dare he make her sound like she belonged in the loony bin! He crooned to her, "It's okay, sis. Shhh, we'll get you home, and you'll feel nice and safe, okay? Come on, sweetie."

When he tried to help her to a standing position, she screeched at him. "What the hell are you doing, Vlad? There's nothing wrong with me." It drove her batshit crazy to see that her date, who she desperately wanted to get rid of anyway, believed every word Vlad said. Who was this joker?

Vlad gave Johnny another sympathetic look. "It's okay, Zoe. I'm going to take you home." He excused them both and dragged her to the door.

When they were outside, he walked her over to his car and pushed her into the passenger seat. He was banking on her wanting to avoid a scene. He won, but once they were away from the pizza shop, she let him have it.

"What are you doing? I swear to God, Vlad, if you ever do that again, I'll twist your balls so hard you won't walk right for a week. Do you understand me?"

Vlad looked at the anger showing on her face and busted out laughing. She was so tiny; it was hard to take her seriously. He had more than six inches on her and at least eighty pounds. His face quickly got serious and drained of all color when she lunged at him while he was driving.

She grabbed his junk in a vice grip. "Oh, no more laughing? Listen clearly, Vlad. One more time, *one* more, and I'll twist these guys off. Do. You. Understand. Me?"

Vlad coughed and asked her to remove her hand. "Yes, Zoe. I understand you, okay? I'll just take you home." He dropped her off and made his way back home. He was actually surprised she was so mad at him. Surely, he gave her enough warning that he wasn't going to let her date other men.

Date number two wasn't much better. He was a nice guy, a blind date who someone at work had set her up with. But completely boring. She almost fell asleep twice before they even got their salad.

"So you see, when there are still worms in the dog's feces, even after de-worming, you know there are other problems. What we do is get more samples of their poop, and…"

"Oh, God. Please. Enough, Zach. I can't take anymore. I can't eat with you talking about dog poop, okay?"

Out of the corner of her eye, she saw Vlad staring at her from the corner booth. How the hell did he know where she was all the time? When he saw that she had caught a glimpse of him, he raised his glass to her in a toast, and went back to looking at his menu with a satisfied smile on his face.

Finally, Zach got off the subject of dog crap and talked about his family. He really was a nice guy and adored his sisters and mother. His father was gone, and he had assumed the role for his sisters years ago.

"When my dad died, it was just something I knew I had to do. I really didn't think about it, you know?"

"I actually do know. Both my parents died when I was young, and I became more of a mother to my little brother." Zoe never regretted a moment of it. Of course, she wished it had been different, but she and her brother, Aidan, were very close. She was thankful for him every day.

Just as he grabbed her hand and started rubbing her palm with his thumb, Vlad came over.

"Oh my God! Zoe Millis!" He leaned down and gave her a sweltering kiss. "I had no idea you lived around here now. How's our little girl?"

"Huh? What little girl?" Zoe had no idea where he was going with this one.

"What do you mean, 'what little girl?' Our baby! You know the one, don't you? Oh, wait, do you have more? I mean the one you wouldn't let me see until I got out of the joint. Well, I'm out, sweetheart. Take me to see her." He reached out and ran his finger down her cheek and right over her breast.

"Vlad, go away." *Kill him*. That was what her brain kept telling her. *Kill him*.

He leaned down and whispered so that only she could hear. "I told you I would interfere. Every damn date—each and every one. Deal with it." He pulled away and licked her lips. "God, you still taste better than anything. Yum." He looked at her date and winked at him. "Enjoy her, she's a wildcat in the sack." He turned to Zoe and told her he'd look her up and call her.

Her third and final attempt at dating ended similarly. Vlad showed up at the movie theater where she and her date went.

Each time Jason attempted to put his arm around her, Vlad would kick his chair. He'd apologize profusely, of course, but he'd do it again and again, until Jason finally gave up.

About halfway through the movie, Zoe excused herself to run to the ladies room. She grabbed Vlad on the way out.

"You are driving me insane. I mean it. Stop following me. How the hell do you know what I'm doing all the time anyway? It's creepy."

Vlad stood there, again thinking how cute she was when she was mad. He put his hands in the air in surrender. "Hey, I'm just trying to protect you. These guys you're seeing aren't good enough for you."

That was the last straw. She'd said it before, but that was it. "And you are? You say you love me, but do you? What is love to you, Vlad? Tormenting a person? Not allowing her the chance for happiness? Is that love? If it is, then you can keep it."

The look on her face rocked him—like someone had taken the wind out of her sails. Had he done that? She covered her face with her hands and let out a breath. "Please stop, Vlad. Please. If you really care for me, just stop." She walked past him and went back into the theater. Vlad couldn't help but notice how Zoe's arms hung at her sides in weariness. He knew he'd caused that.

Zoe stopped dating. Not solely because Vlad was being an ass, but also because she really didn't want to anymore. It seemed like a good idea to simply throw herself into the dating pool, but it wasn't working. Life was not that easy.

Vlad felt like a complete ass. He was so glad that Zoe was done trying to date. He'd lucked out that none of her dates recognized him. He wore hats and glasses and other things to try and disguise himself, but he never knew who might be a Scorpions fan.

He didn't see Zoe for days. It was glaringly obvious she was avoiding him, and he really couldn't blame her. At that point, he had sunk so low, he wished he could avoid himself.

Chapter 8

Vlad had another appointment at the medical center in town—the one he shouldn't be going to as it wasn't a part of the organization. His hip was simply not right; it went out at odd times and was fine when he thought it would falter.

The doctor had run some tests, and Vlad was there to get the results. The news was not good. Dr. Culp wasn't one to sugar coat things.

"I wish I had better news for you. I consulted with a few colleagues, and we all agree. You have avascular necrosis. Basically what that means is that your blood is not getting to where it needs to be in order to keep your bones healthy in that hip."

Vlad hated to hear it, but it made sense. He'd had many injuries to his hip during his career. Years ago, there would have been no chance of fixing him, but now there were possibilities.

The doctor continued, trying to ignore the look of distress on Vlad's face. "You're going to need surgery. The sooner the better. The longer you put it off, the worse your condition will get."

Vlad was shocked. He had assumed there would be a medicine he could take or physical therapy he could do to fix it. Surgery was out of the question. Nostrils flaring, he lashed out at the doctor. "Are you fucking serious? I can't have surgery now. It's the beginning of the season!" He wanted to hit something, throw something. He needed some kind of physical outlet.

"Vlad, I know this isn't what you wanted to hear, but the end of the season is months away. I wouldn't suggest waiting. It looks as though you've also had arthritis in that hip for quite a while now."

"Well, yeah. I can't really remember a time when my hip didn't bother me some. Goal tending's not the easiest position in the world. So, what are my choices here? If I get the surgery, will it cure me? How long will it take until I get back to being a top goalie?" Vlad didn't want to shorten his season, but if that was what he had to do in order to save his career, he'd do it. The biggest issue at the moment was that his contract was up at the end of the season. Who would want to hire a goalie that had missed most of the previous season with hip injuries? It was a tough market, especially for a thirty-eight year old. At that age, his prospects wouldn't be as lucrative as they once were.

"Your last MRI showed the change in your bone marrow. I'm sorry to say, it's pretty extensive. You've got a lot of damaged bone on that hip that won't be able to heal on its own. It needs surgery, Vlad. You'll have a slow recovery, but you're a very healthy young adult. There's no reason you can't get nearly full range of motion back in that hip."

"Nearly full range? Doc, you're not answering the most important question. How long will it be before I can play again after surgery?" Vlad was so fearful of the answer that his breathing was getting rapid, and he was gripping his hands hard enough to turn his knuckles white.

"Vlad, I'm sorry. I don't think you ever will. Not professionally, anyway. You have extensive damage in that hip. Now, you can ignore my advice and play through it, but if you damage more of the bone, we'll need to reconstruct a larger area and possibly ruin the quality of the rest of your life. The sooner we take care of this, the more range of motion you're likely to get back." The doctor walked over to Vlad and put his hand on his shoulder. "I'm sorry, son. I know this isn't the answer you were hoping for."

With a dazed look in his eyes, Vlad shook the doctor's hand. "I'm going to need a while to think about this. I guess I'm going to have to talk to the coaches and staff. I'll need copies of my records for them to look at." Vlad had no idea how he was going to broach the subject with them.

"Of course. Good luck."

Vlad's vision blurred as he made his way to Zoe's house. He wasn't even sure why he was going there, but he was just so angry, he didn't want to be alone. He should still have had a good couple years of playing left in him.

When he got to her house, he didn't bother knocking. Opening the door, he quickly made his way to her office at the back of the house. The door was closed, but he yanked it open anyway.

Zoe sprang up from her chair, hand flying to her chest. "Vlad! What are you doing? I'm with a ..." She stopped dead when she saw his face. He was white as a ghost, and his eyes were suspiciously red.

The Scorpions defenseman, Matt Johnson, stood up. "It's okay, Doc. I'll catch up with you later." He clapped Vlad on the shoulder on his way out. "I won't tell anyone I saw you here, man. Let me know if I can do anything for you."

Once they were alone, Vlad went to Zoe and pulled her into his arms. His voice cracking with emotion, he mumbled words that she couldn't understand. His face was buried in her neck, and he had a death grip on her. She couldn't bear to push him away.

"Shhh. It's going to be okay, Vlad. Please, tell me what's wrong. Let me help you." Zoe gently stroked Vlad's back as he regained his composure.

God, it felt so good to have her touching him. He could almost forget what the doctor had told him. When he started running his fingers through her short hair, he started losing control. "Oh God, Zoe. I need you so bad." He pulled back and captured her lips. "Please don't push me away, not today."

Zoe felt the lump in her throat before she could analyze her own feelings. He needed her, and she needed to be needed. "I won't. I won't push you away today."

Vlad kissed her until she had to pull away just to breathe. "Please let me make love to you. Help me forget, just for a little while. Please, Zoe, make reality go away. Let me get lost in you."

She couldn't think of anything but the feel of his lips against hers. She must have muttered something affirmative, because he picked her up and carried her to her room.

He groaned as he stumbled once on the stairs.

Zoe gasped, the sound of his pain giving her pause. "Are you okay?"

"Shhh, not now." He continued the trip up the stairs a bit more carefully. He reached her bedroom and placed her in the center of her bed. The way he looked at her, like she was the most precious thing he'd ever laid eyes upon, was Zoe's undoing. She reached out to him and pulled him down on top of her.

He braced himself on his elbows and simply looked into her eyes. "You know I love you, right? This isn't just a fling for me. I want it all with you, Zoe." He was actually trembling with his need to make her understand how much he needed her.

Zoe wrapped her hands in his shirt and pulled him down closer so she could kiss his lips. She started out gently, just nibbling on his bottom lip, but when she felt his hands roaming over her she tried to deepen the kiss.

"No way. Not yet, you little vixen. I've waited too long to have you again. I'm going to savor every minute." He sat up and took off his shirt. His jeans, socks, and shoes followed.

Zoe looked at him, lips parted, eyes shining with desire. She pointed to his briefs—low-rise trunks, her favorite—and licked her lips. "I think you forgot something." When she reached a hand out to him, he grabbed it and pinned both over her head.

"Nope. Patience, Zoe." He began slowly unbuttoning her blouse. Each button undone was followed by a kiss—all the way down to the last one. When he licked tiny circles around her belly button, she sucked in a quick breath.

"Vlad, come on." She was reaching for him again.

"Am I going to have to tie you up, Doctor?" He'd be good with a yes or no; either would be highly satisfying.

"If you don't get me naked in about two-point-three seconds, yes, you will. I want to feel your skin against mine. Now, take off my clothes!"

"I love your feistiness. I love that you bring that to the bedroom, but for now, how about you just shut up for a while, huh?" He took the decision away from her by putting her mouth to better use.

While he was kissing her, he ran his hand up her leg and under her skirt. She opened for him and he slid his thumb over her, making her squirm, seeking more.

"Yes, Vlad, right there."

He continued kissing her lips, her neck, the top of her chest, until he got to her breasts. Her breasts weren't large, but she had beautifully pink nipples. They tightened into pebbles under his tongue. When he sucked hard, she thrust her hips up into him.

"More. I want more." She started pushing his head down toward her most sensitive spot. Never let it be said that Zoe was shy in the bedroom.

Vlad let out a laugh. "Anything you want, doll." He relieved her of her skirt and panties, and sat back on his heels to look at her. "You are so amazingly gorgeous." He didn't give her time to reply. He was on her almost immediately. He licked her softly, applying just the right amount of pressure. It took no time at all for her to fly apart that first time, clenching around his tongue.

"That's it, Zoe. Come for me." He gave her soothing licks, but as soon as she started to come down, he started on her again.

"Oh God, no. It's too soon." Zoe tried to wiggle away, but he held her hips firmly. Even though he lightened the pressure of his tongue, he wouldn't stop completely. It was so intense; she didn't know if she could handle it.

"Vlad, oh God. Vlad. Yes. Jesus, yes." She held his head as he kept at her. When he used his teeth on her clit, she came again. Hard. "Yes, fuck, yes. God, don't stop." He again licked her until she settled.

She was panting as he moved away from her, sitting back on his heels. "I need to be inside you, Zoe. Now." He stripped off his briefs and was inside her with one quick thrust. He groaned, long and loud. "Fuck, you're tight."

As he began to move, Zoe had a fleeting thought about condoms. She knew he was clean because she was privy to his medical records, and when he bit her earlobe as he moved faster and harder, she forgot about birth control entirely.

"I'm sorry, Zoe. I'm not going to last very long this time. Too. Fucking. Good."

Zoe ran her tongue up his neck and nipped at him. She widened her legs and grabbed his ass pulling him in tightly each time he thrust. "Just a little bit more, I'm so close." It was amazing. She'd never come so many times before, in such a short period. Vlad really knew how to work her body. "Yes, that's it. Please, don't stop." It was the most intensity she'd ever experienced, an almost punishing rhythm. "Fuck. Harder. Yes, faster!"

Vlad felt her squeeze around him, and he came hard. It felt like the longest orgasm he'd ever had. He kept pumping into her as she called out his name, but as he slowed his movements, he didn't withdraw. Putting his forehead to hers, both of them still panting, he asked, "Is this a bad time to ask if you're taking birth control?"

Zoe laughed. "Yes, this would be a bad time. I am, but I don't always remember to take my pill. We might want to use condoms next time."

"You feel incredible, you know that?" Vlad didn't want to move, but he knew he had to be crushing her. With reluctance, he rolled to the side. He pulled her with him and told her to get some rest. "You're going to need it. In an hour or so, I'm going to make you scream in the shower. Think you can handle that, Doc?"

The smile on Zoe's face assured him she was up to the challenge. "I think I can handle anything you give me, Impaler."

They didn't make it downstairs until well after dawn the next morning.

As they were sitting at her kitchen counter, Vlad told her his story. He hadn't talked about any of it through the night, spending all his time loving Zoe. "What am I going to do?"

Wetting her lips, she got ready to tell him exactly what he didn't want to hear. "Well, I think you know what you need to do."

He raked a hand through his hair, trying unsuccessfully to keep his cool. "Goddamit Zoe! Don't fucking psychoanalyze me!

Just tell me what to do!" He knew he was out of line, but he didn't know what to do with all of his pent up anger. Well, he knew *something* that helped, but they had to take a break to recharge at some point.

Zoe tried to calm him. "I'm not, sweetie. I'm not trying to, anyway. I just don't see that you have much of a choice. Finish the year and possibly hurt yourself beyond healing, or call it quits for this year and see what the next brings." Realistically, Zoe knew that if he made the decision to have the surgery soon, his career was over. He was a thirty-eight year old—thirty-nine by the end of the season—goalie, with a contract that expired at the end of the season. She knew he was well aware that there weren't too many teams looking for a goalie his age coming off a hip surgery.

Vlad's breath came out in a rush. "Shit, this sucks, Zoe." His voice broke, and he turned away. She pretended not to notice, and he continued, "I'm not smart like you. I never did well in school. If I'm not a hockey player, what the hell am I? What do I have to contribute? Who am I? Fuck! I just don't know what to do. Tell me what to do." The way he stood there with his hands stuffed into his pockets, his head down, not even looking at her, was heartbreaking.

"Vlad, you know I can't tell you what to do. Only you can decide that. But if you're asking for my opinion, based on what you told me, I'd play one last big game, give it my all, and then have the surgery. Maybe you could try being a bit nicer to Cage, too. As much as he razzes you, you *are* his mentor. Surely you see that. You've had over sixteen years in the NHL, Vlad. That's pretty damn impressive. Maybe it's time to start a new chapter in your life." Zoe didn't want to mention that she could then be a part of his life if he retired. She didn't like to think of herself as a consolation prize.

Vlad released a pent up breath, raking his fingers through his hair. "I know you're right. I guess it's just going to take some time to get used to. I'll talk to the coach tomorrow. I really want to play the Halloween game. Then I'll retire." Zoe could almost hear Vlad's teeth grinding in anguish. "I can't believe I just said that. I'm actually going to retire." It really would take some getting used to. What the hell would he do all day? "Thanks for listening, Zoe." Vlad finally gave her a playful smile. "And for the *other*."

"The other? The *other*?" How dare he call incredible sex with her, 'other'! Zoe flew at him and almost knocked him off his stool. Laughing, he grabbed her and held her tightly, his breath hitching in his throat. She was the one bright spot in his life at that moment; he never wanted to let her go.

Chapter 9

The next morning at practice, Vlad pulled the coach aside in the locker room and asked if he could have a minute of his time before they hit the ice. Talking to Coach DeLeon was even tougher than he imagined. He hardly knew where to start. First, he had to come clean with the fact that he went behind the organization's back and saw another doctor. Then he had to apologize for not playing at top form when they had lost a couple of their games. Lastly, he had to admit to himself that he'd let his entire team down because of his own pride. It was a hell of a day.

He told him everything. After he heard it, he doubted the coach would let him play again, but he had to try. "I'd really like to play the Halloween game. After that, I'll call it quits and have the surgery. I give you my word that if I'm not up to playing the whole game, I'll pull myself out. I won't let the team suffer for my bad play again."

Coach DeLeon was still trying to digest everything Vlad had told him. "You know our doctors are going to want to check you out themselves. Will you willingly make yourself available for that?"

"Of course. I'll do anything you want me to do. I really am sorry, Coach. I guess I was afraid of finding out exactly what I found out. My hip has always bothered me a little. I just thought it was the life of a goalie, you know? I already got copies of all of my records from the medical center." Vlad took a large file out of his bag and handed it to the coach.

Frustration evident by his tension-filled expression, Coach DeLeon took the file. "Okay, Vlad. I'll give this to Dr. Vane. Halloween is only a couple of days away. Go suit up and get out there. Practice with the guys for a while and see how you feel. I'll leave it up to you whether to tell them or not. It's your decision. If you decide not to, we'll have a meeting after the Halloween game."

"You're going to let me play?" Vlad couldn't help the feeling of elation that washed over him. Knowing it could be his last game ever would make it the most special game of his life.

"I am, as long as you give me your word, on your honor, that you'll pull yourself out if you can't give me one hundred percent."

"I swear it, Coach. You have my word." Vlad was humbled by the coach's support. "Thank you."

Practice went better than he expected. Before Vlad could enter the locker room afterward, Dr. Vane grabbed him. "Come to the training room with me for a second, would you?"

Vlad followed him down the hallway, wondering how pissed he was that he had gone to the medical center. When they reached the end of the hallway, they turned right and went into the first training room.

Dr. Vane threw the folder down with enough force to spill some of the papers. "Want to explain this? You have one of the best medical teams available to you twenty-four-seven. Not everyone is lucky enough to have that kind of experience and expertise at their beck and call, yet you went to the medical center for a hip issue. Does that sound about right?"

Immediately, Vlad could feel his body tensing up. He tried to remind himself that he did, in fact, go behind their backs. Anyone would be angry about that; however, he was not some errant child to be talked down to.

"Look, Doc. I've already apologized to Coach. I'm sure he explained the situation to you. It was nothing personal about the care your team gives us, okay? This isn't about you. Try to understand that."

Dr. Vane seemed to back down a bit, slightly cooling off. "Fine, let's move forward. I've reviewed your test results and spoken to Dr. Culp. Unfortunately, I agree with his findings and his course of action. I'm not pleased that you went to him, but I am sorry this is a career-ending situation." Vlad could tell Dr. Vane was upset; he'd always had an amiable relationship with him. "I can imagine it's going to be hard to hang up your skates, but you're actually lucky you caught it in time. You should be able to play hockey again, just not on a professional level. Make sure you do all of the therapy required afterward. You're young and in good shape, so you should come out of the surgery well enough."

"Yeah, okay. Thanks." He walked out of the room feeling worse than he did before. He didn't mean to step on the doctor's toes, which he obviously did, but he didn't appreciate being pinned as the bad guy either. He was dealing with enough as it was.

When Vlad left, Zoe called Lacey. "Hey Lace, how are you today?"

"Hungry—same as every day. I'm almost five months pregnant, and I've gained fifteen pounds. From what I've been reading, I'm already about five pounds over what I should have gained at this point. I have a doctor's appointment tomorrow. We'll see if I get in trouble."

Zoe thought she looked exactly like she should. Healthy, but rounder. "Well, how about if we pig out today. I'll help you plan a better diet tomorrow if the doctor says it's necessary. What do you think? What do you feel like?"

"You know what I could go for? Some Mexican food. Extra, extra spicy. If I call in an order, will you stop at La Esperanza's? I made pineapple ice cream last night, so we can have that for dessert." Zoe could practically hear Lacey's stomach grumble through the line.

She tried to keep her laughing to a minimum. "You're making your own ice cream now, too? Is this the same girl who yelled at me for not getting enough vegetables at the grocery store when you lived with me?"

"Hey, I'm eating for two! As sweet as Jody's been, he gently suggested that maybe it would be easier to buy an ice cream maker instead of him constantly running to the store at odd hours."

"Sounds logical. Okay, order me some General's chicken. I'll be there soon."

It took Zoe two trips to bring in the food and drinks. She had stopped at the store and picked up a few of Lacey's other pregnancy-inspired favorite foods too.

Lacey was poking through the bags when Zoe returned with the last bag of food. "Ick, I don't eat pork rinds anymore. God, they're disgusting. I don't know what I was thinking."

"Jesus, Lace. You loved them just last week. You're a mess." Zoe took the pork rinds and set them aside. "Still into these?" She held up a value-size jar of stuffed cherry peppers.

"Oh my God, yes. Let me get some plates. You can open them now if you want."

As they were eating their array of food, Zoe got down to the topic at hand. "Okay. There was a specific reason I wanted to come over here today. I need to talk to you, but you have to promise not to get mad."

"I can't promise I won't get mad, Zoe. What did you do?"

Zoe took a deep breath and looked Lacey directly in the eye. "Vlad and I spent the night together last night. And it wasn't the first time." Zoe typically didn't give a shit what anyone

71

thought of her. For the most part, she was pretty tough. Lacey was different, though. Lacey had her respect, and Zoe couldn't stand it if she thought less of her, which was why she'd never told her about her first night with Vlad. "I'm sorry I kept it from you, but I don't ever want to disappoint you. I guess that sounds stupid, but you're the one person I need to be proud of me."

"Oh my God. Okay." Lacey's eyes widened. "Wait! Was *he* the OCD guy you were with that night you called me when I lived in Maine?" At Zoe's affirmative nod, Lacey continued, "I always wondered what happened to that mysterious guy, but it was beyond obvious that you didn't want to talk about him. I just figured he did something crappy and you were done with him."

Lacey took another bite of a cherry pepper along with some of her enchiladas. She pointed her fork at Zoe while she kept talking. "You know, thinking back, I remember how happy you sounded on the phone that day. You loved him even then, didn't you?"

"You're not going to chastise me? Sleeping with the players and all that? You seemed to have plenty to say about it back then. And you didn't even know that I'd slept with one." Zoe sat with her hands together, waiting for Lacey's answer.

"No, I'm not going to chastise you. You know what you did was wrong, and you did it anyway. I'd say that speaks volumes. Zoe, you're a good person with a strict set of moral and ethical codes. I'm not going to judge you for falling for the wrong guy." Lacey put her hand over Zoe's when she didn't say anything else. "What are you going to do about it?"

Zoe bit her lip and looked around the room, stalling for time. It was a shitty situation, and she didn't even like thinking about it, let alone talking about it. Responding slowly, she started to tell her about Vlad's upcoming surgery. "It's not going to be an issue for much longer. Vlad has to retire." Zoe was surprised to feel her eyes burning. She believed everything she had told Vlad. He'd had a great career, and was more than likely nearing the end of it anyway, but that didn't make the fact that it was not by his choice that he had to retire any easier.

"Wow. I did not see that coming. Is that why he's been such an asshole lately?"

Zoe instantly felt angry on Vlad's behalf. She was now firmly in his corner, and she would defend him. "Maybe *asshole* isn't quite fair. He's been a bit edgy, but he's had reason to be, okay?" Seeing Lacey smile, Zoe smiled herself. "Yes, I feel defensive of him, happy? It's not like you didn't know how I felt about him. Anyway, he's got a hip disease and is going to need surgery. The longer he waits to have it, the worse it will get. He'll probably still be able to play again someday, but he'll never be like he was. He'll never play professionally again."

"Holy cow. How's he taking that bit of news? I know it was hard for Jody to retire, and *he* did it by his own choice. Hockey gets in their blood. It's how they define themselves."

"I think he's taking it okay. He has his moments, of course, but all in all, he seems like to be dealing with it. I think his biggest concern is what he's going to do afterward. He about broke my heart when he came over yesterday. He had actual tears in his eyes." Seeing big, tough men like Vlad cry wasn't something you saw every day.

"Oh God. That must have been tough to witness. Poor Vlad. Did he tell the team yet? Does Jody know?"

"He's talking to the coach today. He hasn't told Jody yet either. I know it's asking a lot, but could you please not tell him? I didn't ask Vlad if it was okay to tell you, although I think he'd assume I would." Zoe knew that if she asked Lacey to keep quiet, she would.

"Of course. I won't say a word." Lacey grabbed Zoe's hands. "You know, there is one silver lining here."

Zoe smiled. "Yes, I do. I'm not sure Vlad's even realized that yet, but he sure did a fine job of showing me how he feels last night. Five times to be exact. Well, five times for me. Only three times for him."

"Sounds like a hell of a night. I miss those nights. I run so hot and cold lately. Last night I wore poor Jody out, but last week I almost bit his head off for trying to touch me. The man really is a saint."

Chapter 10

After Vlad talked to the coach, he shot Jody a text asking him if he was done for the day and had time to talk. Jody worked as the head coach for the youth team that the Scorpions' owner had started. They used the second rink in the same building the Scorpions practiced in, so he knew Jody would be around somewhere.

Vlad was sitting on the picnic table in the back parking lot when Jody strolled out. "Hey Jody, how are the kids looking?"

The kids came from all over the area. Some were only able to be there because they were sponsored by the Scorpions' Wives Club. They were a non-profit organization who helped out anywhere they could, but mostly with children. The youth league gave kids a chance to stay out of trouble while building team skills. They also got the chance to learn life skills, such as hard work and tolerance of others, from great mentors, like Jody. Unfortunately, a lot of the kids didn't have any of that at home.

"It's going pretty well. The kids are great to work with. They're so enthusiastic, and I think a lot of them are just relieved they have somewhere to go after school."

"I'm sure their parents are, too. So listen, I wanted to talk to you about why I've been such an asshole lately."

Jody stood there, obviously waiting for him to continue. "I figured there was a reason. People don't change personalities the way you have without one. So, what is it?"

"You know how I've been a little sore lately? Falling on the ice? Almost falling the night of your wedding?"

"Yeah. I noticed."

"Turns out I have avascular necrosis. It's a career-ending disease for me. The Halloween game will be my last. I'm going on long-term injured reserve for the rest of the season, and then I'm done. I'm going for a surgery consult a couple of days after the game."

Jody stood immobile, stunned into silence. After Vlad's words sunk in, he rubbed his hands down his face. "Holy shit, man. I'm really sorry to hear that. I sure didn't expect you to say that. I don't know what I thought it was. I guess I just figured it was Zoe."

Vlad told him the rest of the story and what the doctors had told him about the likelihood of him playing professionally again. "I'm not ever sure I'd want to come back if I couldn't be one hundred percent. At least this way, I can go on LTIR so my salary doesn't affect the cap. Then they can hire another goalie." As he was talking, Jody got a peculiar look on his face. "I know that face. You've got an idea or something. Spill it."

"Well, I was just talking to Mr. Clark about filling another coaching position. I'm one man short. I was actually thinking about looking for a goalie coach and overall help with the defense. What do you think?"

"I don't know. I mean, I know I'll need to do something, but I haven't gotten that far. I have no idea how long it's going to take me to get back to skating after the surgery. What if it takes months, or what if I never get back on skates again? Fuck, man! This is some scary shit." Vlad had to admit, though, the idea was intriguing. It definitely had merit, but how could he expect Jody to hold a position open for him when he couldn't ensure he could do the job?

"Tell you what. Why don't you just worry about the surgery, and let me talk to Mr. Clark? I've been operating without the extra coach for a while. I can hang on for a while more until we know what you're dealing with. Are you even interested in something like that? I can tell you that working with the Mini Scorpions is a hell of a lot of fun. They're good kids. Well, most of them."

Vlad pulled Jody over for a one-armed man hug. "I think it sounds like I have some thinking to do. But yeah, talk to Mr. Clark, and let me know how he feels about it. We'll go from there. And thanks a lot, Chief."

Zoe had missed three calls from Vlad while she was seeing clients. Hoping nothing else had happened, she quickly called him back.

"Hello, gorgeous," Vlad answered on the first ring. It seemed he was feeling better than he was earlier. She knew it would take time for him to accept the situation, but there was nothing he could do but learn to live with it.

"Hello yourself. You sound pretty chipper. I'm glad. I was a little worried when I saw you called three times."

Vlad laughed. "Well, I've finally got you where I want you. I don't want to give you a chance to change your mind about us. Plus, I was wondering what you were going to wear to the Halloween game. Can I assume it'll be something skimpy like last year?"

"I'm not telling you; it's a surprise. And Vlad, I'd still like to keep our relationship quiet until everything is finalized, okay?" Zoe was aware that everyone already knew how they felt about each other, but until Vlad was officially retired, she wasn't comfortable declaring them a couple.

He was glad to hear that she finally considered them to be in an actual relationship, but he was ticked that she still wanted to keep it quiet. "Oh, come on, Zoe. It's just a few more days. Are you seriously telling me that I'm going to continue to be your dirty little secret until I'm officially retired? Technically, I'll be on LTIR until the end of the season. No way. Good luck with that." He was done waiting.

"Why is it so hard for you to understand how important my job is to me? Your job is important to you. And your career is ending without your say, so you know how that feels. Why would you want something to compromise mine? If you have such strong feelings for me, why can't you wait a few more days? 'Good luck with that?' Don't be an asshole, Vlad. *I* still *have* a job to worry about!"

As soon as those last few words slipped out, Zoe slapped her forehead. *Shit, shit, shit.* At Vlad's silence, she ran her hand over her face feeling ashamed. "Shit. I'm sorry, Vlad. I didn't mean it like that. I mean I *did* mean it, but that was incredibly insensitive. I'm just angry. Frustrated" There was more silence, which made her wonder if Vlad hung up. "Vlad?"

"Angry, huh? Well guess what? I'm angry, too. You're the only good thing I have going right now. At least after the other night I *thought* I had you. Looks like I made a mistake—again." Vlad ended the call and wouldn't pick up when she called him back.

Jody and Lacey were finishing up dinner that evening when their doorbell rang. Izzy, their dog, let out a sharp bark, but didn't bother getting up.

"You're such a great watch dog, Iz." Jody gave her a pat on the head as he stepped over her one hundred forty pound body to get to the door.

Zoe stood on the other side, looking out of sorts. "Hey, Zoe, come on in. Lace's in the kitchen."

Zoe walked over to the seat next to Lacey and sat down hard. "I fucked up." She laid her head on the table with a dull thud. "I fucked up bad. I think I can fix it, but I'm scared. Jody? Beer, please."

Lacey sat there and watched Zoe all but chug her beer. "Well, what happened?"

When Zoe was done telling her, she cocked her head in thought. Her lips curled slightly as she stared blankly at the bottle in her hands. Zoe loved what she did for a living, but did it have to come at such a high cost? Finally, she had the mother of all epiphanies. "You know what? If I get fired for being with Vlad, I can find another job. Know what I can't find? Another Vlad."

Zoe put her career before everything else in her life, and she knew that was why Lacey seemed so shocked. While she was normally fun and carefree, never taking anything too seriously, that wasn't the case when it came to her career. When suicides became much too common in the NHL, it affected her. She wanted to do something to prevent that lethal combination of over-medicating and depression from ending in suicide. After two years of being with the Scorpions, the players finally trusted her and were comfortable enough to open up to her. She felt confident that they would come to her for help if they needed it.

"I don't know what to say, Zoe. You know I'll support you whatever you decide, but I can't weigh in on your decision. It's too big, and it's yours to make, not mine. For what it's worth, though, you are right about one thing. There is only one Vlad Bejsiuk."

Zoe put her hand over Lacey's. "I know you have my back. And I know what I'm going to do. To hell with everything. This one's for me. Go big or go home, right?"

Vlad was just stepping out onto the ice when Zoe walked into the rink. He didn't see her, but she wasn't surprised. It was Saturday, and practices were free and open to the public. She guessed there were upwards of two-hundred people packed onto the metal bleachers surrounding the practice rink.

She made her way down to Vlad's end of the ice and yelled loud enough for her voice to carry over the glass wall. "Hey, Impaler!" No response. She banged on the glass and tried again. "Come on, hot stuff! Turn around for me!"

At his caller's second yell, Vlad's face broke out in a grin. He simply couldn't help himself. He knew that voice, and he couldn't stay mad at her. He'd tried.

Vlad slowly turned around, lifting his mask. With an eyebrow raised and a smirk on his face he asked, "What do you want, sweetheart?"

Zoe was suddenly very nervous. It was one thing to think about throwing caution to the wind. It was quite another to follow through with it. And now, most of the team was on the ice as well. She took a deep calming breath and went for broke. "Marry me!" *Oh shitballs. I meant to say, 'I love you.' Where the* fuck *did that come from?*

It got so silent on the ice, she could actually hear the lone puck that was skating towards Vlad's net. And that was quite a feat for a rink filled with people. Vlad took off his blocker and glove. Then he removed his helmet and placed everything on top of his net. Skating over to her, he said loudly, "Why do you want to marry me?"

She didn't have a ready answer. Could she take it back? No. Did she even want to take it back? *Crap, crap, crap. Keep calm. Think!* She began to realize it was actually exactly what she wanted. She'd been in love with him for a long time, and he with her. Now that they were finally able to move forward, why not skip the whole dating thing? She wasn't a twenty year old kid who didn't know what she wanted. She knew what she wanted. She wanted forever—with Vlad.

"Do we really have to yell at each other through the glass with all of these people watching and listening?"

Vlad crossed his arms and laughed out loud. He nodded his head. "I think after all this time, I deserve it."

Zoe was so happy to see Vlad's eyes sparkle in amusement like they used to that she didn't care about her surroundings anymore. "I want to marry you, because I think you're the bee's knees."

He quirked his eyebrow at her again. "Bee's knees? Nah, try again, woman. Dig deeper."

She even liked annoying Vlad. Rolling her eyes and grinning like a mad woman, she gave him another reason. "Well, you're not too bad on the eyes."

"That's a little better. How about something a bit more substantial?"

"All right. How's this?" She took her time to make sure she picked the right words. Vlad *did* deserve to hear how she felt. He *did* deserve the public recognition of her feelings for him. She put her hands up against the glass. "The first time I see you each day, you take my breath away." She rolled her eyes at herself for using such a cliché phrase and tried again. "I thought about what it would be like without you in my life and it hurt here." Zoe placed a hand over her heart. "You and me—we fit." With a cocky smile, she finished, "And let's face it: you've been smitten with me from the first time we met."

"Wow, is that right? You're not very humble, Dr. Millis. Luckily for you, I happen to find that an attractive quality. Plus, you're right. I have been." Vlad waved her down the glass to the door that opened onto the ice.

He opened the door when she got there and pulled her into his arms. He lifted her so that she was standing on his skates. He skated out to the center of the rink, keeping a firm hold on her as he lowered her to stand next to him on the ice. Intertwining their hands, he addressed the crowd. "Should I marry this woman? What do you think, does she deserve me?"

There were cheers and boos alike. The naysayers were definitely the puck bunnies who had a thing for Vlad.

"So? Don't keep a girl waiting." Zoe looked into his eyes and brushed back an errant curl that was hanging over his eye.

"I would love to marry you. You've already got my heart; you might as well have the rest of me."

Zoe kissed him softly. "Thank you," she whispered.

Chapter 11

Vlad was anxious as hell. The start of the Halloween game was less than four hours away. He prayed to all the deities he could think of that he'd have his best game ever.

He was already at the rink, leaving Zoe to go the game with Jody and Lacey. He had left earlier than usual to get his head in game mode. Before every game, he sat in the empty arena, helmet in his hands, staring at the ice. His ritual had begun as simply a way to clear his head and get in the zone. When his win record started getting better and better, it became a superstition.

Matt, the defenseman who was in Zoe's office when Vlad barged in, climbed the stairs toward him. "Hey, man, how you doing? You're here even earlier than usual, aren't you?" Matt always got there early, too. He liked to do a light workout before games.

"Yeah, I'm just taking some extra time to clear my head." He didn't want to tell the guys that it was his last game until after the game. They didn't need to be thinking about him when they should be thinking about getting the puck in the net.

"Well, I won't bother you too long. I just wanted to congratulate you again. We're happy for you and the doc. Are they going to fire her, though?" None of the guys wanted to get used to another therapist.

"Nah, I don't think so. We'll have to see what happens. So far, no one has said anything." Vlad had actually talked to Mr. Clark, the owner of the Scorpions. He told Vlad that they would overlook it, due to the circumstances.

"We all hope they don't make her leave, man. She's great. You deserve her." Aside from Vlad's attitude the past six months or so, all the guys genuinely liked him—even Cage. He was one of the older team members, and they looked up to him. "All right, Impaler. I'll leave you to it. See you in the locker room." With a slap to Vlad's shoulder, Matt jogged back down the stairs into the tunnel leading to the locker room.

Zoe shook her head as she looked at the costumes that Jody and Lacey were wearing to the game. Lacey's costume was a far cry from the sexy fallen angel she was last year.

Jody was going as Charlie Brown, accompanied by Lacey dressed as Snoopy. Lacey was wearing a white shirt and white pants. Her baby bump was Snoopy's face. Black floppy ears, sewn to the sides of the shirt, hung down on either side of her big belly.

Zoe doubled over, laughing. "You have got to be kidding me. I am not sitting next to you two." She wouldn't be caught dead in something like what they were wearing. Halloween was a time to break free. It was a day to wear something that you couldn't get away with on a normal day. She had tried to talk Lacey into going as a scantily dressed trailer park girl, complete with a fake cigarette hanging out of her mouth, but she seemed to have lost some of her influence on Lacey since she had married Jody. Too bad.

Zoe's costume, on the other hand, was an eye catching number. No cute Snoopy for her.

"Jody—put your tongue back in your mouth please." Lacey gently put her hand to Jody's chin and shut his mouth for him.

Zoe smiled and spun around. She was dressed as Daisy Duke from *The Dukes of Hazzard*. Her barely there Daisy Duke short shorts were matched with a red button down shirt that she'd tied in a knot to rest under her breasts. The first four buttons were undone, and her red fuck-me-heels were the perfect accessory to make the outfit really stand out. "You like?"

Jody looked at Lacey, alarm clearly showing on his face. "I have no way of answering that question without condemning myself." He kissed Lacey and walked out of the room shaking his head. "Vlad is not going to like you wearing that, Zoe!"

"Don't you think Vlad will like it? I mean, I look hot, right? I don't think he'll mind. He never minded before when I smutted it up for Halloween." Zoe hadn't even given that a thought. Not that it would matter. She'd wear what she wanted to wear.

"Yeah, but you weren't his before. Well, we'll find out soon enough, won't we?" Who knew how Vlad would react. He wasn't exactly himself as of late.

Vlad saw Zoe in the stands during warm ups and immediately felt his groin tighten as he took in her costume—what little there was of it. When he lifted his mask and nodded his head in approval, she gave him a sexy smile he knew was all for him. He tugged on his jersey and swiveled his hips trying to rearrange himself before putting his helmet back on to skate back over to his goal.

"Looks like he approves." Zoe would have worn it either way, but it was a bonus that he didn't freak out like Jody would have if Lacey wore something like that.

"Approves? Yeah. I think you'll be getting a lot of use out of that outfit." Lacey hooked her arm through Zoe's. "Come on. Let's go up to the box. Jody's getting nachos. He said he'll meet us in there."

Zoe blew Vlad a kiss and pretended to drop something so that she could bend over for him. She saw him laughing as she threw him one last look over her shoulder. *Good luck*, she mouthed to him.

Detroit usually came out like gangbusters, but you never knew how a team would play from one game to the next. This game started out slowly, which was good for Vlad. It gave him a little extra time to stretch out and determine how his hip was going to affect his play, if it even would.

With a little over six minutes left in the first period, the score was still zero to zero. One of Detroit's instigators decided to try and shake things up by getting Marcoux to drop his gloves. Brandon was not a fighter. He was a twenty-two year old winger who weighed about one hundred and seventy pounds soaking wet. It was a joke.

When Marcoux refused to drop his gloves, Cooke shoved his stick up hard into his face, cutting his lip open. That definitely took things to the next level, but certainly not in the way Cooke had wanted. He went to the sin bin to serve a four-minute major penalty, which allowed the Scorpions to score on an extended power play. A couple of minutes later, the period was over and the Scorpions would go into the second, up a goal.

In the locker room during intermission, Coach DeLeon pulled Vlad aside and asked him how he was feeling.

"I'm doing okay, Coach. I'm still good to start the second period. The pain is only about a three. You okay with that?" His pain was probably closer to a five, but he wanted to finish his last game, and the pain wasn't affecting his play yet.

The coach looked at him for a second, eyebrows raised, before responding. "A three, huh? So what, that's really about a five? You look good. I can live with that." He clapped him on the back. "I trust you, Vlad. I know you'll pull yourself out before you would hurt the team. Have a good second period." He walked into the center of the room to give the team a pep talk, and off they went to start the second.

Pucks were flying up and down the ice so fast in the second period that, at times, the spectators were struggling to keep up with the action. Both teams had upped their intensity and physical play. Bodies were bouncing off the boards, and pucks were flying toward both nets. Vlad was getting a hell of a workout and was feeling the effects.

"A little help here would be great guys! Can I get some fucking defense?" Vlad just needed thirty seconds of rest. Christ, if he could just get thirty seconds where he could stand still. *Goddammit! I'm gonna have to pull myself out of this game if they can't keep the fucking puck away for a minute.* His hip was so sore and weak; he knew it was just a matter of time before he went down.

Zoe wasn't enjoying the game at all. Knowing what she did about Vlad's hip condition, it was painful to watch him constantly going down into the butterfly and then snapping right back up to protect the high spots. He had to be in agony.

Two minutes away from the end of the second period, it happened. Garvey, one of Detroit's bigger centers, had the puck and was bearing down hard on Vlad. The Scorpions were in the middle of a sloppy line change that left only one defenseman in between Garvey and Vlad.

Vlad was ready for him. In his peripheral vision, he saw Keith racing down the ice to help defend the goal. They were almost upon him. There were four of Detroit's players and only two Scorpions, plus Vlad. He didn't like those odds, but he was ready.

Just as Vlad decided that Garvey was going to shoot high, he decided to go for the money shot. Right through the five hole. Vlad quickly slapped his pads together, going down to cover the space. He thought it was over, but Garvey's skate went out from under him, and he slammed into Vlad, landing on his leg, bending it back at an awful angle.

"Get the fuck off me! Goddammit!" He threw his glove and blocker off and pushed frantically at Garvey. Keith lifted him off and pushed him away.

"Shit! You okay, man? You want me to call the trainer?" Vlad didn't look like he was getting up anytime soon. He was now on his hands and knees, moving his legs back and forth in the grips of pain like he'd never felt. It almost looked like he was crawling.

"Fuck. Yeah, I'm done." Never in his life had he felt like that. Not when he broke his nose, not when he burnt three layers of skin off his leg on a muffler as a kid, never. He lost his battle with the pain and flopped onto his back, trying not to pass out.

After a minute or two, Keith and Matt helped him up. He gingerly lifted his right leg up to take the pressure off his hip. The other Scorpions pulled Vlad off the ice on one skate. The crowd cheered out of respect for him, which was nice, but that was not how he wanted his last game to end. He didn't know if he wanted to break something or cry.

Zoe couldn't stand to watch Vlad withering in pain on the ice. She didn't know what to do. All she wanted was to be with him, but she knew she wouldn't be allowed back in the training room.

"Oh my God, Lacey. How did you stand this when Jody got hurt?" Jody had left to see if he could get any answers about Vlad's condition. "Text Jody and see if he knows anything yet." She knew she was being ridiculous; he had just walked out the door.

"Zoe, you know …"

Zoe put her elbows on her knees and her head in her hands. "I know, Lace. He probably isn't even down there yet. Fuck. I hate this!"

"Hey. Come on, Zoe. He'll be okay. I mean yes, it looked very painful, but he'll be okay. He didn't get cut or hit in the head." Lacey squeezed her neck. "He'll be okay."

Zoe took a deep breath and stood up. "Okay. You're right. He'll be fine." She stood up suddenly. "But I have to go down there. I have to wait for him or anyone, down there, okay? I just need to be there."

"Sure. I'll go with you."

The security guard wouldn't let them into the locker room. Not even Lacey, but he told them he'd go get Jody for them. He turned to do just that, and Jody walked out.

"I only saw him for a second before the trainer threw me out. They're putting him in the whirlpool for a bit, but he'll be okay. Well, as okay as he can be with that hip of his. He asked me to take you home, Zoe."

Vlad was still in the training room, soaking in a whirlpool, when the buzzer sounded, ending the game. There was a TV in the room allowing Vlad to catch the rest of it. Cage pulled off a stellar performance. He'd be lying if he said it didn't rankle him a bit. He wanted Cage to be great for the team, he did, but it was still a blow to his pride.

Speaking of the bastard, Cage sauntered into the room to see how Vlad was feeling. In typical Cage fashion, he started out his conversation with an old man comment. "Can't hang with the young guns anymore, huh, Impaler?" He looked back and saw that the TV was still on. "I see you caught the game. You see my saves? You better be afraid, old man. It's just a matter of time until I'm in the number one spot."

"Fuck you, Booker. Don't you ever know how to talk to people like they're not shit on the bottom of your shoe? I'm doing fine, thanks for asking." Vlad was in no mood to deal with that cocky little shit. In no mood at all. Vlad tried to stand up and get out of the whirlpool, but went back down as soon as he put weight on his bad hip. "Shit!"

"Whoa. Dude, let me help you. I'm sorry, man. I didn't realize how badly you were hurt." Cage walked over to him, but stopped about a foot from the whirlpool at Vlad's look. He obviously did not want his help.

"Just go back to the locker room and celebrate with the team, would you, kid? I'll be there in a few." When Cage left, Vlad let out a weary sigh as he gingerly lifted himself up again. He was able to get out and get himself dried off. After he dressed, he limped his way into the locker room. He was about to tell the team that he had played his last game.

"Hey, Vlad. How you feeling, man?" Keith came over to him as soon as he saw him walk in. "Here, have a seat. That looked like a nasty position to go down in. What's hurt, your leg?"

"Not really. I'd like to talk to the team for a couple of minutes before the celebration really kicks in. Think you could get their attention for me?" Vlad just wanted to get it over with at that point.

Keith paused in the middle of removing his elbow pad. Vlad knew he was intrigued. "Yeah, sure." Keith whistled for attention. It took a couple of minutes and another whistle and shout, but they finally quieted down. "Hey guys. Vlad wants to talk to us for a second. Listen up." He turned to Vlad. "They're all yours."

"Well, first of all, good game. Sorry I couldn't finish it with you." Vlad looked down at his feet. He knew he was stalling, but if he said it out loud, if he finally told them he had to retire, it would really be true. He was leaving the NHL. He'd never play pro hockey again. *Fuck, that sucked.*

He looked out at his teammates and took a deep breath. "This is tougher than I thought it was going to be."

Keith walked over to him. "Just say what you need to. We got your back, man. We're family here."

Vlad could feel that nagging burn behind his eyes again. These guys really were his family. "Thanks, I know it. Okay, I guess I'll just cut to the chase. Tonight was my last game. I'm retiring at the end of the season, but I'll be on LTIR for the rest of it." There were sounds of shock and denial going around the room.

"Is that why you've been such a foul bastard lately?"

Derek, the equipment manager, slapped Cage in the back of the head. "What the hell is wrong with you, Booker? You need a serious attitude adjustment." Cage had been getting on everyone's last nerve lately. The better he did in net, the worse he got.

"What? I'm just saying what everyone else is thinking."

Keith had had enough of Cage for the moment. "Ignore him. I know I will. Now, what do you mean this is your last game? What's going on?"

"I have avascular necrosis. It's a bone disease, and it's currently residing in my right hip. I'm having surgery soon to replace the damaged bone. I'll be able to suit up again someday, but my pro hockey days are over." There, he said it. And—he was okay. Not great, but okay.

"Wow." Keith looked everywhere but at Vlad. "I—I don't know what to say." He ran his hand through his hair and looked Vlad in the eye. "I'm really sorry, man. You've given everything you have to this team. You've been our number one goalie for years. You've held records in the league for a couple of them. We'll all feel the loss." Going for a little levity, he said, "Although, that little fucker ..." He pointed to Cage. "Will probably be happier than a pig in shit."

Cage clearly took offense to that and whipped his head around to address the whole room. "That's not true. I know I screw around a lot and say the wrong things now and then, but I'd never wish any of you harm. Yeah, I want to be the number one goalie, but I wanted to earn it." Cage walked over and shook Vlad's hand. "All kidding aside, Vlad, you've taught me a lot. You're a great mentor. We'll all miss you in here."

"Thanks, Booker. You just make sure that you work as hard as you can to support this team. I'm not just going to disappear. If you start fucking up this team, you'll still have me to deal with, got it?"

Cage smiled. "Yes sir, Impaler, sir. Good luck with your surgery."

"Thanks." After receiving well wishes, condolences, and a few snide remarks about hurting his hip on purpose so he could 'bump uglies' with the hot doctor, he took his leave.

Zoe was waiting for Vlad by his car. She'd been standing there for over an hour, and her feet were killing her. She was also getting a bit chilly in nothing more than her skimpy shorts and top. When Vlad finally limped out, she noticed he didn't seem too pleased to see her.

"Hey, Zoe. Why did you wait for me? I thought Jody was taking you home." Vlad obviously wanted to be alone. Or she thought he did anyway. She hoped seeing her standing there in her hot little shorts made him rethink that, even if he was tired as hell.

"Are you serious? You didn't think I'd want to be here for you after the game? Especially after you got hurt? How are you feeling?" He'd hounded her for years, and now he didn't want her around? What the hell?

Vlad shook his head at her, exasperated. "Christ, do you have any idea how many people have asked me that? How am I supposed to answer? I'm fine? I feel like shit? My hip hurts so fucking bad I could cry? Which one would make all of you feel better?" There he went again, being an asshole.

Zoe walked over to him and took his keys. "I'm going to give you a slide on the attitude. I'm sure you've been playing nice in the locker room long enough. Go get in the car. I'm driving."

"Nuh uh. No one drives my baby but me. She's a classic. No way." Vlad tried to grab the keys back, but she wasn't giving them up.

"Yes, Vlad. I can recite it in my sleep. Everyone can. She's a 1969 Camaro Z28. Supercharged. Three-point-five inch exhaust mufflers and some other stuff. Bottom line? She's a car. Get in." Zoe walked around to the passenger's side and held the door open while Vlad stared at her in disbelief.

"Not just 'supercharged,' Zoe. She's got six hundred sixty supercharged horses ready to gallop under that hood." Vlad was pointing at the hood as his voice rose. He was seriously defensive of his car. "She's more car than you can handle. Give me the keys. Now." He held out his hand expectantly, but Zoe just laughed at him and got into the driver's seat.

When she turned the key, the engine roared to life. She had to admit, it did sound incredible. It truly was an awesome piece of machinery, and by the sound of it, Vlad had finally gotten all the bugs worked out of the engine. The white racing stripes on the bright blue paint sparkled, but it was still just a car. She stepped on the gas pedal, making it roar louder. Zoe raised her voice to make herself heard over the noise. "You coming or not?"

Vlad carefully slid into the passenger's seat and gave her a look that would make lesser women cower. "I swear to Christ, Zoe. If you get one scratch on Louise I will throttle you—throttle you!"

Zoe swung her head toward him. "Louise? That's my middle name."

"Yeah, I know. Let's just go, okay? I want to take the meds the doctor gave me and try to sleep. I have an appointment with the surgeon tomorrow." He obviously wasn't in the mood to talk, so they drove to his place in silence.

When she pulled into the underground garage, Vlad realized that he'd need to take her home. "You should have driven to your house. Why are we here? You're not taking my car home."

"I'm not going home." She opened the door and got out, leaving Vlad still sitting in the car. Rolling her eyes, she walked around and opened his door. She bent down, giving him a fabulous view of her breasts, and asked him if he was coming.

Not yet. He continued to stare at her breasts for a few seconds before answering. "Yeah. Okay. I'm really tired, though, Zoe. I just want to go to sleep."

Zoe smiled, shaking her head at him. "I got it, Vlad. You don't have to worry about me. Your virtue's safe for tonight. Come on. Just this once, let your guard down, and let me take care of you. Let's go."

Vlad looked at the steps leading to the elevator with unease.

"Six steps, Vlad. That's it, just six steps." At the top, Vlad heaved a sigh of relief. They got into the elevator, and he ran his security key over the panel to take them up to the penthouse.

Once inside, Zoe followed him into his bedroom.

"What are you doing? I told you—" Vlad stopped mid-sentence. Zoe was undoing the knot in her shirt. "Zoe?"

She continued to unknot her shirt as she peeked up at him through her lashes. "Hmm?" He wanted to relax? She knew a great way to help him relax.

Vlad swallowed hard. "I said: 'what are you doing?' I—I thought I was going to take my meds and go to sleep?"

"Take your meds and lay down. Don't argue, just do it."

He was captivated enough to follow her orders without further question. It only took him a minute to go into his bathroom and take his meds. He'd thrown his shoes off on his way back into the bedroom and was about to unzip his pants when Zoe stopped him.

"Let me."

Vlad looked up at her and saw that her shirt was gone. As were her shorts. She was standing in front of him in a red lace bra, red thong, and her red stilettos. He wanted to freeze time so that he would have that vision of her forever in his mind. *Incredible!*

"Jesus, Zoe. You are so gorgeous. I want you so much I can't think straight." He took a step toward her, letting out a heavy sigh as he reverently ran the back of his fingers down her cheek. "God, I want you, but I honestly don't know if I can tonight."

Zoe had her hands on his zipper and could feel him bulging out of his pants as she carefully lowered it. "Oh, I think you can, Vlad." She cupped his length as she slid the zipper all the way down. "And, from the feel of things, you want to as much as I do. So, the only question here is how creative do we have to get?" She licked her lips as she continued to stroke him. "I can do creative, Vlad."

She walked him slowly backward, until his knees hit the bed. Putting her hands on his chest, she gently pushed him back until he was lying down. Then she carefully shimmied his pants off, mindful of his sore hip with each move she made.

He scooted himself up farther on the bed while ripping his shirt up and over his head. Zoe followed him and pushed him back down again. Throwing her leg over him so that she was sitting astride him, she said, "I think this will work just fine, don't you?" As long as he didn't move too much, she wouldn't even have to be that creative. What a shame.

Vlad wasn't sure he had enough blood in any part of his brain to form a coherent thought, so he simply nodded his head in agreement.

Laughing in triumph, Zoe gently rubbed herself against his hardness. "Oh, that feels good. Is that okay?"

"Uh huh."

"Let's lose the rest of our clothes, shall we?"

Vlad propped himself up on his elbows and watched as she leaned over, pressing herself against him. She didn't leave an inch between them as she slid down his body pulling his briefs off along the way. He enjoyed watching her undress him, but it was nothing compared to watching her undress herself. The heated look in her eyes as she unhooked the front clasp of her bra told him she was a woman who knew what she wanted. There was no shyness in her moves. No hesitation. As she peeled her bra off, she allowed her hands to brush over her sensitive nipples, letting out a low moan.

"That feels good, but not as good as your lips." She climbed her way back up his body and got close enough for him to have a taste of her. "Ahh, that's better." She allowed him a quick minute to nibble and lick her breasts before she pulled away and stood up to take off her thong. Standing at the side of the bed, she turned around giving him her back. She hooked her thumbs in the sides of her thong and ever so slowly slid it down, bending over and wiggling her ass as she did so. When she reached for her shoes, Vlad broke his silence.

"Leave them on." His voice was rough with desire. She felt her insides clench at the rough, raspy sound.

Without saying a word, she straightened up and got back onto the bed. She threw her leg over him, and quickly but gently took him deep inside her until she couldn't tell where she ended and he began. Neither one of them wanted to take the time for foreplay. It was one of those times when she simply had to have him inside of her as soon as possible. She was more than ready for him. "Am I hurting you?"

"God, Zoe. I'm fine, just fuck me."

Zoe loved making love as much as fucking. There was a time for each, and the time for fucking was upon them. She gave him more, and when she was sure she wouldn't hurt him, she rode him hard until they both exploded in ecstasy.

Hours later, both perfectly sated, they were still awake, talking about getting married.

"You seemed kind of surprised that you asked me to marry you. Are you sure that's what you want, Zoe?"

She reached for his hand and locked their fingers together. Turning her head she looked into his eyes so that he could see the truth in them. "To be honest, I meant to say 'I love you', but 'marry me' came out. I did freak out internally for a couple of seconds, but then I realized it felt right. You know, sometimes the heart knows what it wants before the head understands it.

I'm sure, Vlad. One hundred percent sure. I want to watch you get old."

"Me get old? What about you?"

"I'm a woman. I'll dye my hair and wear tons of makeup. I'm not getting old."

He smiled at that and traced his finger down the new pink stripe in her hair. It was subtle, but he loved it. She definitely had her own style. "You'll always be beautiful to me, whether you're thirty or eighty."

"Well, no shit. I'm pretty hot." She winked at him and brought his hand to her lips. "I'll always find you irresistible too, you know. Even if you have two bum hips."

Vlad's hand tightened in hers. "God forbid! Don't even joke about that. I'll need at least one good hip to keep up with my hot wife. You're very demanding in bed you know."

Zoe sucked on his finger and he let out a groan. When she bit the tip, he pulled his hand away and pulled her onto his chest.

Absently stroking her hair, he asked, "When can we get married? How long do you need to plan everything?"

"You know how I am. I'm not a fancy person, Vlad. I don't want a big wedding. I'd be happy with just you, me, Jody and Lacey in the court house. Then we could just throw a kickass party."

"Are you serious? You might just be the perfect woman."

Zoe laughed and slapped his chest.

"Seriously though. You don't want the big wedding? Lots of people? The frilly dress?"

"No. I don't. It's just not me, Vlad. What do you want?"

"That's easy. I want whatever you want. I want you to be happy."

"Good. Then let's tie the knot around Christmas time and get er done!" She kissed his chest and stifled a yawn.

"That sounds perfect to me. Now let's get some sleep. We'll talk more tomorrow, okay?" Zoe didn't answer him as she was already half asleep.

Zoe woke up a few hours later and watched Vlad sleep. The pain medication he'd taken was working, and he finally looked relaxed in the luxury of a pain-free sleep. Gently running the tip of a finger over his slightly parted lips, she thought about how they had come together.

She loved him so much it scared her. It was a miracle that she had been able to hold him at bay for so long. Zoe had never truly believed in soul mates outside of movies and literature. Surely there was more than one person in the world who could be someone's other half. But looking at Vlad lying there, she couldn't imagine ever loving someone else like she did him. As guilty as it made her feel, she couldn't help thinking that his injury was her blessing.

It wasn't quite dawn when Zoe quietly got out of bed and headed into the shower. Using Vlad's soap and shampoo, borrowing his clothes—that were ten times too big—and just feeling secure in his love, were comforts that Zoe hadn't enjoyed since before her parents died and her life fell apart. Being in his home with him made her feel like maybe she really could have it all. Maybe she didn't need to be quite so independent. Maybe it was okay to finally let someone take care of her.

Less than an hour later, Vlad woke up to find Zoe missing. He made his way downstairs and found her wrapped in a blanket on the patio, watching the last of the sunrise.

Vlad stood inside, hand on the door for a full minute, drinking in the sight of her before making himself known. She turned at the sound of the door sliding open and leaned back in the lounge chair, watching him as he joined her on the patio. He walked over to her with a brilliant smile on his lips as he rubbed his arms in the cool morning air. "Good morning."

Zoe smiled up at him, and his first thought was that the sunrise had nothing on her smile. She spread her legs and opened her blanket, scooting back on her chair. "Come on in here and get warm."

He sat down and she wrapped her legs around him, pulling the blanket tight over his chest. "How's your hip feel this morning?"

"It's okay."

"Really?"

Vlad sighed. "No, not really. It hurts enough that I'm not hating the idea of having surgery as much today. It's going to take me a while to get over the fact that my career is over, but this hip seems to be getting worse all the time. I don't want to live in pain, so I guess the surgery seems more like a blessing than a punishment at the moment."

"Wow. Sounds like you've been doing some hard thinking. That's good, Vlad." She kissed the back of his neck. "Try not to worry about what you're going to do after the surgery. Just worry about healing. The rest will work itself out."

"I know it will. I'll make it work. I know Lacey told you about the possibility of my working with the youth league. I think I could be good at that. Some of those kids need role models, and hell, if I didn't kill Cage, how bad can those kids be?" First, though, he had to get through the surgery.

Chapter 12

Zoe went with Vlad to see the surgeon to discuss his procedure. His entire family was in Ukraine, and she was adamant that he didn't go alone.

Vlad had told his parents he was retiring, but he didn't go into too much detail as to why. They knew he had hip issues, but not the extent of the disease. He'd eventually have to explain it all to them, but thought it would be best to have more information before doing so.

They were sitting in the waiting room when Vlad started fidgeting—picking up magazines, shuffling his feet, gripping his hands. He was obviously more nervous than he let on. He had come to terms with the fact that his career was over, but that didn't mean he wasn't worried about what the surgeon was going to tell him. He reached over and gathered Zoe's hand in his, resting them on his thigh.

"Thanks for coming with me today." He rubbed his thumb back and forth over the back of her hand. "It's nice to have you here. I didn't really want to do this alone, but, you know, I'm such a tough guy and all." Vlad flashed a quick smile at her that was clearly laced with fear and uncertainty.

"There's nowhere else I want to be." She gave his hand a reassuring squeeze. "I'll hold your hand, take the brunt of your anger over this, or sit silently while you process your thoughts. Whatever you need."

He didn't deserve her. Truly, he didn't. He had been such a prick of late. He knew how great Zoe was, but it was humbling to see this gentler side of her. She was such a tough girl, but wow, when push came to shove, she could provide tenderness and support like no one he'd ever met.

He didn't have words like she did, so he just leaned over and kissed her cheek. "Thank you."

"Mr. Beggsiack?" The receptionist cleared her throat. "I'm sorry, Mr. Beg—" She smiled at her own inability to even guess how to say his name. "Vlad?"

Vlad gave her a genuine smile. He knew his name didn't flow easy. "Good enough, I know it's a good, strong Ukrainian name, right?"

"I love unique names, but I sure can mangle the pronunciation." She offered him a smile and pointed toward the door. "The doctor will see you now."

The interior room they were shown to was decorated with bunnies and ducks on lively yellow wallpaper. "Is this their way of lightening up bad news? That's not a good sign."

Zoe was as surprised as he was. It wasn't the décor one typically saw in a surgeon's office. A pediatric office, sure, but a surgeon's who replaced hips?

The doctor came in and shook Vlad's hand. "Sorry about the room. We're doing renovations so I've been using this children's room for consultations. So, how are you feeling today, Vladimir?"

"Just Vlad. Vladimir's my father." And his father before him, and his father, and so on. "How am I feeling? I'm not sure how to answer that. Are you looking for a pain scale?" He wanted to give the doctor as much information as he could to get the best help.

"Just overall. Tell me what you're feeling. I saw the game last night. Getting your leg bent back like that couldn't have been pleasant. How were you treated for it?"

"After I was over the danger of puking from the pain, I sat in a whirlpool for a while. Took some pain meds last night and went to sleep." Vlad stole a quick look at Zoe remembering the part in between that he wouldn't dare tell the doctor. Zoe answered with a smile that told him she knew exactly which part he was remembering.

"Good. And how are you feeling today? Is there any relief from the pain?"

"Some. I don't think I'd want to strap on skates, and I'm still limping a bit, but I can take it. I would say the pain is about a five. I haven't taken any pain pills today because they make me too loopy. If I don't need them, I don't want them."

"That's fine. You don't have to take them right now, but I would like you to take some anti-inflammatory pills when you have pain. They'll help without simply masking the pain and making you tired. Okay, on with the bad news."

Shit. How could there be any bad news left? Vlad looked over at Zoe. She wore the same surprised expression that he did. He grabbed her hand once more. "Uh, bad news? I thought I got that already."

"Well, you got some. I was looking over your most recent MRI, and I believe your damage is worse than Dr. Culp originally thought. I talked to him, and we discussed what I saw. I believe we're looking at a total hip replacement."

Vlad already knew that, didn't he? "Yeah, wasn't that what I was told?"

"Well, no. We were hoping to graft bone from your lower leg to put it in your hip where the diseased bone is. It would have been a longer recovery, but better in the long run. We were hoping the bone would fuse together, get stronger, and that would be that."

"Okay, so why is a total hip replacement worse than that, if it has a shorter recovery time?"

"You're young. Chances are you'll have to have it done again. And of course the older you are, the slower you'll heal. It's not the end of the world; it's just a bit more than we were hoping you would need."

Vlad was actually relieved. He thought they were going to tell him he had cancer or something awful like that. "Okay, I can handle that. I'll still be able to strap my skates on though, right? I mean, I know I won't play pro again, but there's this possible job I could have as a coach."

"Absolutely. You'll be able to do almost everything you could do before. I don't think continually going down into a butterfly and snapping back up is something you should do too much of, but you'll have full range of motion."

"How long until I can skate again? What's the recovery time?"

"You're looking at about six to eight weeks, depending on how fast you heal. Some physical therapy will help too."

"All right. Let's get this done." Vlad wanted it done as soon as possible so that he could figure out exactly what he would be capable of doing.

The day before Vlad's surgery, Zoe got a surprise phone call on her business line.

"Hello, this is Dr. Millis."

"Hello, dear. This is Emma Bejsiuk. I'm Vlad's mother. How are you?"

Zoe was taken aback by the beautiful English accent. She was also surprised that Vlad didn't tell her his mother would be calling. "Oh. Hi, Mrs. Bejsiuk. I'm fine, thank you. How are you?"

"I'm doing well, thank you for asking. I'm sure you know that I'm calling to talk about my son. First, let me tell you how glad I am that he has you near. He's insisting that I not come over there for his surgery. He said that you would take care of him, but I would hate for it to be an imposition on you, dear."

Zoe felt warm and tingly inside simply because Vlad had told his mother she would care for him. That was a pretty big deal in her book. Men always wanted their mothers when they didn't feel well. No matter how old they were, it seemed they all turned into little babies when they were sick or hurt. "Oh, no. He's not imposing at all. Mrs. Bejsiuk, I'm really sorry, but I'm going to have to cut our conversation short. I didn't know you'd be calling, and I have a client due in any minute now."

"Oh, that's just fine. I'm sorry I interrupted your work day. Why don't you tell me a good time to call you back so that we can chat? Would that be okay?"

"Of course. How about if I call you back after I'm done with my client?" Zoe was glad she'd have an opportunity to collect her thoughts before talking to Vlad's mother at length. Meeting the parents for the first time—or in this case, talking to them—was important, and she was totally caught off guard by the phone call.

"That would be fine. I look forward to it. Goodbye."

Zoe hung up the phone and immediately picked it up again to call Vlad so that she could yell at him for not telling her that his mother was going to call. Right before the call connected, she heard her client ringing her doorbell. *Literally, saved by the bell, Vlad.*

After the session, as Zoe was showing her client out, Vlad pulled up to the curb in front of her house. She watched as he stepped out of his car with only a slight grimace. There were ten steps leading to her front door, and she was mildly concerned about his ability to climb them.

Vlad lumbered up the steps with a small amount of difficulty and took her in his arms, kissing her soundly. "Hello, gorgeous."

Zoe gifted him with a radiant smile as she wrapped her arms around his neck. "Hello to you, too. What are you doing here?"

"I had nowhere else I wanted to be. Want to make me dinner?"

She laughed at him, but nodded her head. "Sure. Let's go see what I have to whip up. You got lucky. I just finished up for the day." Zoe grabbed his hand and led him inside.

"While I'm cooking, how about you tell me why you didn't give me a heads up that your mother was going to call me? Oh, speaking of that, I have to call her back! I almost forgot." Zoe started walking over to the phone, but Vlad grabbed her by the waist, stopping her.

"My mother called you? When? How?"

"You didn't know? She called my office today. She thanked me for looking after you. I could only talk to her for a couple of minutes, because I had a client coming in." Zoe had no idea how much Vlad had told his parents about his condition. Apparently they needed to work on their communication skills.

"Huh. Mom is pretty crafty. Although, how hard is it to Google Zoe Millis, sports psychologist? I may have told her you were the love of my life, but I never gave her your number." Vlad smiled and pulled her against him again. "I talked to them for a while last night and filled them in on everything. My mother kept steering me back to the surgery, but I kept talking about you." He kissed the tip of her nose and ran his hands down her back to cup her bottom.

"Well, I need to call her back before I make dinner. I told her I would. Did you tell her we're getting married?" She pushed herself away from Vlad and made a beeline for the phone before his hands got any more aggressive.

"No, not yet. I wasn't sure if you'd want me to. I didn't want to get in trouble with you if you wanted to tell them." Vlad followed her and wrapped her up again, nuzzling her neck. "I'll tell her when you call her if you want, but you can call her later. I have other plans for you right now."

Zoe felt a shiver go through her at his seductive tone, but she wouldn't be distracted. She told his mother that she would call her back and she would. "No, Vlad. I'm calling your mother back. Then I'm making dinner, and then I'll think about letting you make love to me." She gave him a saucy smile. "But I have to warn you, I'm feeling pretty frisky."

"Frisky works for me, woman. Okay, call my mother. I'm going to grab a beer and sit down if you don't mind." His hip didn't care for standing too long these days.

"Sure. Go sit on the deck. Want anything to munch on while you're waiting for me?"

"Nah. I'll just take the beer." Vlad gave her another quick kiss before he left her alone to make her phone call.

Zoe's talk with Vlad's mother went well. They agreed that Emma would not fly over for his surgery, but Zoe would call her frequently with updates. Unbeknownst to Vlad, they had also made plans for his parents to visit for the upcoming Thanksgiving holiday, which was only three weeks away. She decided they could tell both of his parents then that they were getting married.

Zoe wasn't used to having a big family around. The Bejsiuks were bringing Vlad's aunt and uncle with them, along with his three young cousins. She hoped Vlad would be okay with her offering her home to his family. His place only had one spare bed. They talked it over during a dinner of chicken stuffed with spinach and goat cheese.

"You invited Aunt Anna and Uncle Ruslan? And Sasha, Julia, and Lena? Are you serious? Do you realize that the triplets are only ten years old? Where am I going to put them all?"

Zoe grabbed his hand to stop him from talking. "Your mom and I already discussed it. I have two spare rooms. I told her that you would be happy to buy another bed to put in the third bedroom upstairs. I just use it for storage. It can be cleaned out in a matter of hours. No big deal."

Vlad laughed. "Oh, I see. You're using my family as an excuse to furnish your house." He let out a resigned sigh, shaking his head, but with a smile on his face. He would deny her nothing. "So how long are they staying?"

"I thought you'd be happy to see your family. What's wrong with you?" Zoe punched him in the arm with mock severity.

"I am, It's just …" The way he held his head down, he looked like a pouting child. "It's just that we won't be able to be together. My family will be cock-blocking me! That part kinda sucks."

"Oh my God. Are you serious? Cock-blocking?" Zoe burst out laughing. "You're thirty-eight years old. You can't go a few days without sex, Vlad?"

"It's not funny. I'm thinking about my surgery. I don't know how long it'll take until I can. What if I'm ready the same time my family gets here? You still didn't tell me how long they're staying either."

Zoe folded her hands and placed them on the table in front of her. Softening her voice, she said, "Well, I don't have their exact itinerary, dear, but we discussed them possibly coming the day before Thanksgiving and leaving the Sunday after. That's only five days. I think you can make it."

"Fine, but as soon as they're gone, I'm keeping you in bed for a week—even if I have to tie you down."

Zoe gave him a saucy wink. "Tie me down? I can't wait."

Chapter 13

The day of Vlad's surgery was dreary and rainy—a rarity in San Diego. He was waiting for Zoe in the lobby of his building when she pulled up to the curb at six AM. He waved to her as he made his way to her car.

"Hey, baby." He leaned over and gave her a kiss as he got in.

"Hey. Are you nervous?"

"Not really."

Zoe glanced at him, her disbelief showing on her face. "Not even a little?"

"Maybe a little, but not too much." He could see that she wasn't buying it. "No, really. I'm okay. I want to get the surgery over with so I focus on healing. I'm good, don't worry." Saying it out loud solidified it in his mind. He really had come to terms with the whole situation.

"Good, I'm glad. Okay, let's do it." Zoe put the car in drive and pulled away from the curb.

They got to the hospital in plenty of time for Vlad to get checked in. "Who will be waiting for you Mr. ..."

"Bejsiuk." Vlad pointed to Zoe sitting in the waiting room. "That beautiful creature will be waiting for me. Dr. Zoe Millis." He figured he'd throw the doctor in there, just in case there were problems and she needed the pull to get information.

"Is she a relation?"

Vlad gave the receptionist a dazzling smile that had her smiling in return. "Not yet. My family lives in the Ukraine, so my fiancé over there volunteered to take care of me today."

She was smitten. Vlad's smile tended to do that to women. Putting her chin in her hand, she eyed him dreamily. "So that's where the nice accent comes from." Seeming to suddenly remember that Vlad was a patient, and not her own personal eye candy, she sat up straight and got back to business. "Yes, okay. Please take a seat. A nurse will be calling you shortly."

Vlad grabbed a magazine that he had no intention of reading and sat down next to Zoe. "Well, that's that. Now I wait to get called back."

Zoe grabbed his hand. "You'll be fine. You'll just go to sleep and when you wake up, I'll be there. Then you can start the healing process. Concentrate on that. Just imagine how good it will feel to walk around pain-free again."

Good God, she was going to scream! Vlad had to be the worst patient in the history of the world. Zoe had rescheduled her appointments for the day of and the day after Vlad's surgery to take care of him. Before they even left the hospital, she was regretting it.

He was funny when he first woke up in the recovery room, but it was short-lived. She could tell he was out of it from the anesthesia, because he couldn't stop telling her how hot she was. He also kept asking her—rather loudly— if he'd ever 'tapped that.' The nurses thought he was adorable. Zoe thought he was annoying. To shut him up, she quietly told him that he had indeed 'tapped that'—for the fifth time.

"Daaayyyam, baby. You're so hot. We've really done it?" He tried to grab her arm to spin her around.

Zoe slapped his hand away. "Stop, Vlad. Just drink your juice."

"Come on, just turn around. I wanna see that ass."

"Vlad, please quiet down. We're in the recovery room. Do you remember that you had surgery?"

Vlad scrunched up his face like he was trying to concentrate. "Oh, God. Am I okay? What happened?" He didn't even wait for her to answer him before he tried to grab her again.

When Dillon, the nurse, came in to check on him, Vlad informed him that he'd slept with Zoe.

"You see how hot this girl is? We've had sex. Lots of sex, right? Shit, what was your name again?"

Biting her bottom lip, desperate to get Vlad off the subject of sex, Zoe asked the nurse if Vlad's reaction was normal. "He doesn't seem to remember who I am. He's also single-mindedly focused on sex. And he's not quiet about it."

He tried not to laugh as he answered her. "He's fine. People react differently. Men almost always focus on sex if there's a pretty lady around—anesthesia or not." He winked at her to put her at ease. "You qualify. He's a lucky guy."

"Thanks, but how long will he be like this?"

"It varies. Since he's still so out of it, let's see if we can get him to go back to sleep."Dillon walked over to Vlad and checked his vitals.

"Mr. Bejsiuk? How are you feeling?"

"I feel fucking fantastic. You see my girl? I can't remember her name, but she's fuckin' hot, isn't she, man?"

Dillon ignored his question, but gave him a friendly smile. "How about you do me a favor and take a little nap? It'll help us get you out of here faster and then you can go home with your beautiful girl."

"Yeah, sure. Anything to get to her quicker." Vlad winked at the nurse. "We guys gotta stick together." His speech slurred as his eyes slowly shut.

Dillon motioned Zoe to the area just beyond the curtain. "He should be asleep in a few minutes. When he wakes up again, we'll see how alert he is. You can stay in here if you want."

"Thanks, Dillon."

When Vlad woke up the second time, he was his usual self. He didn't remember being awake previously, but from what he was told, it sounded like he was pretty funny. Zoe didn't to seem agree.

Chapter 14

A day later, Zoe was folding some of Vlad's laundry when he walked up behind her.

"What are you doing? I can do that." He grabbed her around the waist and carefully pulled her back against him, kissing her neck. "Remember, I'm supposed to be up and moving around."

"I know. I needed something to do while you were in the shower."

"If you had joined me in there, like I asked you to, you would have had plenty to do. I had a terrible time reaching my back."

"Your back, huh? I don't thinks so. You're supposed to be up and about, but you're also supposed to limit your hip movement. If you're really that impatient to have me again ..." Zoe ran her finger from his bottom lip down to his belt buckle. "See what your physical therapist says."

"Tracey? If I ask her, she'll tell me I can never have sex again. I've only seen her once so far and I can already tell she's vindictive. All I did was suggest that it might be better for a man to help me with the first couple of sessions. What if I had fallen? Of course, now I know she could hold me up. By pure stubborn will if need be." Vlad had gotten off on the wrong foot with his PT. She didn't seem to take it personally, though, thank God.

"Oh, I like her. She sounds like just the kind of therapist you need. Speaking of therapy, are you ready to go? I want to stop at my house and grab a couple of files on the way."

"Yeah, I'm ready. For the record, though, I think it's stupid that I can't drive for four weeks. It's not like it takes that much pressure to push a gas pedal down."

"Yes, Vlad. Anyone who knows you knows how you feel about not being able to drive. Honestly, get over it. You're worse than a child."

Therapy was the usual fun time he was becoming used to. His drill sergeant made sure he did every single freaking exercise. And she was not pleased if he didn't do them to perfection.

"Come on, Bejsiuk, clench those muscles. My eight year old could do it better."

"Well, maybe if you weren't pinching my ass, I could concentrate. You know I'm taken, Tracey. I think you need to look elsewhere." He clenched his glutes as tightly as he could and grimaced at the sharp pain he felt.

"Yeah, that's another thing, Vlad. Did you take your pain pills today?"

"I don't need them."

"Yeah, you do. It's not unmanly to take your pain pills. If you can't mask the pain enough, you can't properly do your exercises. If you can't properly do your exercises, you won't get your full range of motion back. Didn't you tell me that you want to skate again?"

She knew very well that he wanted to skate again. He let out a breath and hung his head. "Yes, I want to skate again. Fine, I'll take my pills, but only when I'm doing my therapy."

"And when you go to bed to help you relax and heal. Suck it up. It's not forever, but it is important. Now, let's do some hip abductions, shall we?"

"Oh, yes please. I love them so." Vlad groaned as he rolled over onto his side.

She smiled in that evil way of hers. "I know. Fifteen please. Nice and slow."

He knew she took her job seriously, and that she only wanted to help him heal, but God she was a bitch sometimes. "I'm on it." She made him start over—twice.

As the weeks went by and Thanksgiving loomed ever closer, Vlad began to see a lot of improvement in his hip. He supposed he had Tracey to thank for that. She may have pushed him relentlessly, but he knew he wouldn't be as far along as he was if she hadn't.

Zoe was sitting at her kitchen table, while Vlad stood at the window, staring blankly out at the darkening sky. They were supposed to be planning their Thanksgiving dinner, but Vlad's attention was elsewhere. "What are you thinking about so intently over there?"

"I was thinking about Tracey, believe it or not. I think she may be the devil in disguise, but look at how well I move already. I might get her and her family some Leafs tickets. What do you think? Is that too much?"

"I think it's a great idea. I'm sure she's earned them." Zoe smiled at the offended look he gave her.

Eyes wide, eyebrows raised, he asked, "Earned them? Did I tell you how she taunts me when she feels like I'm not working hard enough? She tells me that the Leafs' goalie is the best she's ever seen, and if it were *him* in therapy, she's sure he'd work harder than me." Vlad laughed as he realized her methods worked. He *did* work harder, just to prove her wrong. "I'll be damned. It works."

"Good for her. I know you, Vlad. I've also had you in therapy. I'd be willing to bet you battle that poor woman at every appointment."

Vlad didn't exactly admit to it, but he did shrug his shoulders as he said, "Maybe."

The day Vlad's family arrived was a crisp one for San Diego. The air was cool with a tang of all things autumn riding in the wind.

Zoe had gone all out decorating her house. She said it was to make his family feel welcome, but Vlad thought she again, used them as an excuse to go shopping. It was no secret that Zoe loved to shop.

The stairway leading up to the door outside was lined with large bales of hay. The smell of them reminded Vlad of days spent in his uncle's barn as a little boy.

Pumpkins of all sizes sat on various bales, while others sported strings of leaves in brilliant hues of red, yellow and orange. Standing sentry at the door was a life-sized scarecrow with a beady eyed crow perched on his shoulder.

Vlad got past all of the outside décor only to be assaulted with the interior decorations. He looked around in awe. Zoe had been very busy since the last time he'd been there.

"Holy shit, Zoe. When did you get all this stuff? It looks like autumn threw up in here."

"Really...you don't know the first thing about making a house homey. Your place is full of black granite and chrome. Maybe I went a bit overboard, but it's important to make a good first impression. I want my home to feel welcoming."

"You know, some might say that you're overcompensating because you're not convinced of your own self-worth."

Zoe looked at him, head cocked in thought. She seemed to discount what he said and shook it off. "Wait, I know why you said that. You've been reading my *Psychology Today* journals again, haven't you?"

"Well, I'm bored." Since he didn't have a physical outlet at the moment, he needed something to occupy his mind. He was tired of watching TV and cruising around the Internet, so he figured that learning about Zoe's world would give them something else to talk about. It was only fair. She knew all about hockey, after all. "And you're changing the subject. Do you really think you need all this stuff to make your house 'homey'?" He waved his arm around the room and waited for her answer.

The world's biggest cornucopia sat proudly on the dining room table. It was overflowing with mini pumpkins and gourds of varying sizes and colors. A large brown velvet bow graced the wide-mouth opening, ribbons spilling over the sides.

All of the windows had some sort of decoration on them. The ones in the living room had strings of pinecones and leaves draped in soft folds over the curtains. The windows that didn't have curtains were adorned with gel cling-ons.

It was complicated, but classy. Zoe had a way of making things that could be tacky—like the gel clings—look like a sophisticated design made especially for the space they inhabited.

He still couldn't help himself. He felt his lips turning up as he took it all in.

Zoe saw him looking all around. She also caught the tilt of his lips. "Don't you dare laugh." A reluctant smile formed on her lips as she tried to see the house as Vlad did. "It's too much, isn't it?"

Taking one last look at a couple of black crows sitting on—what else—a pumpkin, Vlad shook his head. "It looks great, Zoe. It really does. My family will love it."

Thanksgiving Day arrived with much fanfare. The triplets were out playing with a soccer ball on the beach, supervised by Vlad's father, Vladimir, Sr. Emma was helping Zoe get her last minute touches on the dishes for dinner, and Vlad was lounging in the living room talking to his aunt and uncle.

Only a little over twenty-four hours had passed since their arrival, and already Zoe felt as if she'd known them forever. They were such a fun loving family.

Dinner was a boisterous affair. The triplets never stopped talking and bickered constantly. Vlad's uncle and father argued about hockey strategies while Emma, Zoe, and Aunt Anna tried to have a civilized conversation, which was next to impossible over the din of the other conversations flowing around them. Vlad couldn't have been happier. He had gone too long without having a chance to visit his family.

He took a minute to think about how good his life was at that moment. Vlad was feeling like a new man. He had an exciting new job to look forward to, his hip was healing nicely, and he'd finally gotten the girl of his dreams. Everything was just sliding into place.

The only problem was, when things seemed too good to be true—they usually were.

Chapter 15

Vlad's penthouse was filled with aromatic bliss. The smells that pleasantly assaulted Zoe's nose upon entering were spicy and fruity with just a hint of savory bacon cutting through the sweetness.

It was the day after Thanksgiving, and Vlad was hosting a late brunch. Zoe had tried to decline the invitation in order to give Vlad a chance to visit with his family alone, but he'd have none of that. "You *are* part of my family, Zoe," he had said, encircling her with his arms. So, there she was—the triplets and their parents in tow.

Sasha, Julia, and Lena were still giggling and talking nonstop … in Russian. Vlad told Zoe that they were talking about how fun the ride over was. He had hired a limo to bring them over to his place. It might have been overkill, but Zoe couldn't fit six people in her car, and he knew the girls would get a kick out of it—and he was right.

"Please speak English, girls. Remember Zoe doesn't speak Russian yet."

There was a chorus of apologies, and off they were again, this time jabbering in English.

"Yet? I doubt I'll ever speak Russian, Vlad."

"Sure you will. I'll teach you slowly, over time, *moya lyubov*."

"What did you just call me?"

Vlad smiled and pulled her close, putting his lips to her ear. "Moya lyubov. It means 'my love' or 'my sweetheart.'" He felt a shiver run down her body as he placed a kiss just below her ear and then let her go.

Emma was calling them into the kitchen to help carry the many dishes that made up their brunch to the table, when the doorbell rang. Vlad walked over, opened the door, and froze. He was staring at a little girl who looked eerily like his mother. Confused, he called back over his shoulder, "Uh, Mom?"

Emma peeked out from the kitchen and promptly dropped the glass casserole dish she was holding, splattering French toast and shards of glass everywhere. "Oh my God. Who is that, Vlad?"

Vlad looked at Zoe, silently pleading for help. His entire family was in his kitchen. All of them. This little girl, who looked to be about seven or eight years old, could only belong to one person.

Zoe walked over to the door and held out her hand to the older man who was standing next to the sullen looking child. "Hello, I'm Zoe Millis. Can we help you?" It was obvious that the girl was related to Vlad, and Zoe could only guess how. It was also painfully obvious that Vlad didn't know what to do. Zoe wasn't exactly sure herself, but he was still frozen in the same spot, hand on the doorknob, looking back and forth between everyone in bewilderment.

The gentleman reached out and shook Zoe's proffered hand. "I'm Thaddeus Blake, ma'am. I'm Carla Bonner's attorney and was a close friend of her father's." He looked at Vlad and gave him a tired smile. "Vlad Bejsiuk?"

Vlad finally unfroze and let go of the doorknob. When he allowed himself another peek at the girl, he couldn't take his eyes off her. "Yes, I'm Vlad."

Those three little words had the girl's lip trembling. She was the saddest little girl Vlad had ever seen in his life. In that split second, he swore he'd do whatever he could to make that sadness go away. His chest hurt with the need to do so. He knew, beyond a shadow of a doubt, that he was looking at his own child. He felt it bone deep. She felt like his. *Carla Bonner— that seems like a lifetime ago.*

Vlad wasn't thinking straight when he moved forward and abruptly pulled the girl into his arms, scaring her with his abrupt hug. "My God. Carla Bonner's your mother." He pulled back just far enough to tilt the girl's chin up so that she was looking at him, her eyes filled with tears. He spoke quietly, trying not to spook her further. "Do you know who I am, little bit?"

She immediately stiffened in his arms. "Yes, you're my father, but I'm not little, and I'm not a bit." She pushed him away and turned to bury herself in Thaddeus's jacket, sobbing like her world was ending.

Vlad didn't have the first clue what he was supposed to do. He looked to Zoe again for guidance. She was a therapist, surely she could help him. "What do I do?" he whispered to her. "I don't know what to do." He'd never felt so helpless.

Zoe tried to communicate wordlessly with Vlad that he needed to get a grip. The poor girl was obviously freaked out, and Vlad's actions weren't helping anyone. She gave him a bright smile, and pulled him back to give the girl some space. "Why don't you both come in? The three of you can use Vlad's office to talk." Seeing the girl take Thaddeus's hand in a death grip, Zoe addressed her directly. "Or maybe you'd like to freshen up first. Would you like that?"

She nodded her head and released Thaddeus. When she took Zoe's hand, she spoke for the first time in a tiny voice. "My name's Crystal."

"It's nice to meet you, Crystal. My name is Zoe." Pasting a confident smile on her face, Zoe led Crystal down the hall to the guest bathroom. "Here you go. There's a clean washcloth in that vanity, if you'd like to wash your face with some cool water." Zoe turned to give her some privacy, but she wouldn't let go of Zoe's hand.

"Could you stay in here with me? Please?"

"Of course, sweetie. Would you like me to wet a washcloth for you?" Zoe didn't wait for an answer; she grabbed a fresh washcloth out of the vanity and ran it under cold water for her. "Here you go."

Crystal stood there uncertainly with the washcloth in her hand. She had her head bowed, staring at the ground, and her shoulders were rounded in a look of utter defeat. She peeked up at Zoe through her wet eyelashes, and in a voice so soft that Zoe barely heard her, she said, "I don't know how to do this."

"Wash your face? Here, honey, I'll do it." When Zoe reached for the washcloth, Crystal looked up at her.

"No. I don't know how to live without my mom." She broke down again. "How? How do I grow up without her?"

Zoe watched with what felt like a vice clamped around her heart as Crystal slid down onto her knees and buried her face in her cupped hands. Zoe immediately sat on the floor with her, holding her tightly.

"Oh, Crystal. I'm sorry, honey. I'm so sorry." Then she just let her cry until there was nothing left.

Vlad and Thaddeus were in Vlad's office where he grabbed a shot of vodka to calm his nerves. "I know it's a little early, but do you want some?"

"No, thank you. That stuff would knock me out."

Vlad immediately thought better of taking the drink in front of his daughter's guardian. *Holy shit, I have a daughter.*

Thaddeus saw his hesitation and put him at ease. "No, you go ahead. I understand you wanting to calm your nerves a bit. Believe me, I've been researching and watching you for almost a year now. I know you don't abuse alcohol."

"You've been watching me for a year? Why? What's going on? Why did I not know that I had a daughter?"

"I felt that Carla was getting ready to tell Crystal about you, and I wanted to make sure you were worthy of her." He taped the folder he was holding. "She left you letters. I'm sure she explained things in them."

"What happened to Carla? Where is she?"

"Carla died of breast cancer almost two weeks ago. I've had Crystal with me since. I kept her with me to get her through the funeral and Thanksgiving Day. My wife thought it was the right thing to do. I hope you're not upset that we didn't bring her to you straight away."

"Upset? How could I be upset? That poor girl lost her mother, and God only knows how she feels about me." He looked at Thaddeus, shaking his head in disbelief. "I can't believe I'm a father. What happens now?" Vlad threw back his shot of vodka and tried to sit down next to him, but his nerves won out. He stood right back up again and paced about the room, running his hand through his hair as they talked.

"Well, I'm hoping that you'll want to keep your daughter. I'm hoping that you'll want to raise her. She's a wonderful little girl, Vlad. She's become quite withdrawn in the past couple of months, but that's to be expected. Carla did not have an easy death. We tried to keep Crystal away near the end, but she would just sneak in and hold Carla's hand as she cried. Carla didn't even know she was there."

"God, of course I want to keep her. I would have wanted to keep her from day one. At least I think I would have. She probably hates me. What did Carla tell her about me?" Vlad had no idea if she painted him as a bad guy or not. Why didn't she tell him she was pregnant?

He remembered meeting Carla at a bar after a game when he played for Vancouver. She was a sweet, petite girl—all sunshine and rainbows. They dated for about six months and then she broke it off. He had thought it was strange at the time, but he just moved on to the next girl. He could remember thinking *screw her, there are tons of girls who want me.* Now, of course, he could see that for what it was. He couldn't say he was head over heels in love with her, but he cared for her, and it hurt when she dumped him.

"She told me that she never told Crystal about you, but she did give her your last name. I'm sure, given time, she would have come to find you. Especially if she became a hockey fan. Bejsiuk, as you know, is not a common name around here."

Vlad pulled in a deep breath and held it. He let it out slowly as he looked up at the ceiling, thinking. "Is there anything I need to do to settle Carla's estate? Is there a house to be sold or debt to be paid? I'll take care of all of that, of course." Thinking about all of the stuff he didn't know was overwhelming. "Shit, I mean, does she have any pets? Do I need to go to Vancouver to get her clothes and stuff? What do I do now?"

Thaddeus got up from his chair and put a hand on Vlad's shoulder. "I took care of all of that. She has some suitcases out in the hall. Carla donated most of the furniture in the house. Crystal's furniture is at our house. We can arrange to have it sent here. There is nothing left for you to do but take care of your daughter." He put the thick folder on Vlad's desk. "Her birth certificate, school records, doctor's notes, and a lot of other records are all in here. I put my card in there with my home phone number, my cell phone number, and my wife's cell phone number. You can call us anytime, day or night."

Vlad looked at the older man with some relief in his eyes. "Thank you. I appreciate it. You were very close with them, weren't you?"

"Carla's father was my best friend for thirty years. When he died, my wife and I stepped in to look after his only daughter. She was scared when she discovered she was pregnant. We tried to get her to tell you, but she was afraid she'd ruin your career, and she didn't want to be responsible for that. You can learn about that from her letters, though. I can tell you this. Maybe keeping Crystal from you was wrong, but Carla didn't have a malicious bone in her body. She believed, until her dying day, that it was the right thing to do."

Vlad looked up at the knock on the door. Zoe stood there holding Crystal's hand. Crystal's eyes were red and puffy, but dry. She stood there with the courage of an adult, lip trembling slightly, head held high, looking at Vlad. "Hi. I guess I'm your daughter. Uncle Thad told me that I shouldn't be mad at you, because you didn't know about me, but I still kind of am."

Thaddeus walked over to her and picked her up. "That's okay, honey. I'm sure your father understands. I know I told you that you shouldn't be mad, and you shouldn't, but it's okay to show your feelings. Just be fair to him and listen to what he has to say. Give him a chance, okay? And remember, you can call me and Aunt Maggie anytime. Day or night." He kissed the top of her head and set her down.

She took a deep breath, straightened up to stand tall, and walked over to Vlad. "Am I going to live here with you?"

Vlad was having a hard time getting past the lump in his throat. "Yes, little ... Crystal. You're going to live with me here. And I'm sorry that I didn't know about you."

"Thank you."

"Do you want to go meet the rest of the family now? We were just going to eat brunch, although I guess we're not having French toast now." Vlad smiled, trying to lighten the moment.

"Okay." She was a girl of few words.

Conversation at the dining room table was strained to say the least. Zoe decided something had to be done, and tapped her fork on her glass of orange juice to get everyone's attention. "Let's make this a better brunch. We are all so lucky today to get to welcome a new family member. Since I don't know anyone but Vlad here very well, let's all just say something quickly about ourselves, shall we? I'll start. I'm Zoe, and I love hockey." She smiled at Crystal, asking if she wanted to go next. Crystal shook her head and glued her eyes back to her plate. Zoe squeezed her hand and said, "No problem. How about you, Vlad? Why don't you go?"

Vlad looked around the table, careful to include Crystal in his gaze, but not settle on her. "I just found out today that I have a beautiful little girl, and I couldn't be happier. I have a lot to be thankful for. Oh—and I like hockey, too." He caught Zoe's approving smile and felt good.

Vladimir spoke up with a heavy Russian accent. "I am Vladimir, and I am lucky patriarch of this family." Looking at Crystal he winked and added, "This means I am biggest, strongest man. You come to Grandpa Vladimir if you ever need to, okay little bit?" He looked away from her then so that she didn't feel pressured to answer him.

"I'm Emma, and aside from being happy that we welcome another little one into our family, I also love animals."

"I am Ruslan. I like to snack on little girls!" He then grabbed Lena and pretended to chew on her arm in rapture as she squealed in delight.

Vlad's aunt Anna smacked Ruslan's arm. "Not at the table, Rus." She cleared her throat and addressed the table. "I am Anna." She looked at Vlad affectionately. "Or Aunt Anna. I love animals, too, and hockey, and new little girls. Welcome, Crystal."

Lena was chosen to speak for the girls. "Hi Crystal. We are your cousins Sasha, Julia, and Lena. And we're sorry that your mom isn't here, but we are very glad to call you cousin." Lena quickly put her head down, not sure if it was okay to mention Crystal's mother.

Zoe put her head down close to Crystal's. "Do you want to say something? You don't have to if you don't want to."

"Okay." She raised her head, just like she did in Vlad's office, and let out the breath she was holding. What a brave little girl she was. "I'm Crystal. I love animals, but I've never watched hockey." She flashed Vlad a quick look. "But maybe I'd like to."

"I'll take you to a game anytime you want, Crystal. You just say the word." He smiled at her and then asked if she wanted some fruit.

Conversation flowed more freely after that, although Crystal didn't say another word.

Chapter 16

Crystal had become quite attached to Zoe by the end of the day. Zoe pulled Vlad aside when Emma had taken all of the children out onto the patio to watch the sunset.

"How are you holding up?"

"God, Zoe. I don't know. What the fuck do I know about raising a child? A girl, no less? Maybe it would be better if I gave custody to Thaddeus and his wife. She seems comfortable around them."

"Vlad! You can't be serious. There is no better place for a child than with a parent who loves them. You'll learn to love her, I know you will."

"Learn to love her? Zoe, I already do. It's been all of what, six hours? It freaks me out. But I don't think she's ready to stay here with me. What am I going to do with her tonight? Have her sleep on the couch? She probably won't sleep a wink. She doesn't know me at all." He banged his fist on the counter. "It's just not fair. No kid should lose their mother so young."

"If it makes you feel any better, it's not much easier at thirteen." Zoe knew what it was like to lose a mother *and* a father. "At least she still has you, even if she doesn't quite know what to do with you yet."

Zoe had been thinking about Crystal's first night in a strange place. "Look, Vlad. I don't want to step on your toes, but I'm only thinking of Crystal. I have an idea."

"Please, fire away. What's your idea? I'm sure it's smarter than anything I can come up with."

"Don't sell yourself short, Vlad. Aside from giving the poor thing a bear hug when she came in, you've been doing great." Zoe was quite proud of him. She didn't know what she would have done if he hadn't welcomed Crystal into his home. "She seems to have taken a liking to me. I think she's comfortable with me. I'm closer to her mom's age than Emma or Anna, and she sees me as a friend. What about if your mom and dad go back to my house with the rest of your family and I stay in the guest room with Crystal? Just for the first night or so to get her settled."

"Yes. Thank you, Zoe. That would work out great." Vlad hugged her tightly. "Thank you for helping me. I know I'd royally fuck this up without you."

Vlad's family took their leave after making plans for everyone to meet back at Zoe's house the next afternoon. Zoe made a quick phone call to Lacey, and gave her a brief rundown of everything that had transpired and then asked her for a favor. "Do you think we could borrow Izzy for a night or two? Would Jody let us?"

"What about your allergies? You know Izzy's going to want to sleep on the bed with you. She doesn't realize she's one hundred and forty pounds. She still thinks she's a lapdog."

"I don't care. I'll take my allergy pills. This poor girl needs something like Izzy draped over her tonight."

"Okay, hold on a sec."

Zoe waited while Lacey checked with Jody. Izzy loved kids, so she knew she'd be happy spending the night with Crystal. Peeking her head around the corner to glance into the living room, Zoe saw Vlad trying to talk to Crystal. She answered his questions, but offered nothing more.

"If it goes like I think it will, Vlad will take her to get a dog tomorrow if she wants one. I really think she needs something of her own to care for. If not a dog, then maybe one of those furry rat things." Zoe was *not* an animal lover. She wouldn't ever hurt one or anything, but she never wanted one in the house. Her allergies were a great excuse to not have any, but they weren't quite as bad as led people to believe.

"I think you might be talking about a guinea pig or a hamster, Zoe. They're adorable, and most definitely not rats."

"You say potato ..."

Lacey laughed. "Okay, fine. So, is Vlad totally freaking out? I can't imagine what that must be like. How could Carla keep that kind of thing from him? I mean, I guess I she had her reasons, but it was so unfair to both Vlad and Crystal."

"Well, Carla didn't see it that way. She left Vlad some letters, but he hasn't had a chance to read them yet. Hopefully,

140

in those, she'll explain why she didn't tell him." Zoe heard a knock at the door and yelled to Vlad that she would get it. "I have to go. Jody's here. Thanks Lace!"

"Call me tomorrow and let me know how it went."

"Will do. Bye."

Before Zoe got to the door, she heard Izzy howl. She couldn't help the smile that tugged on her lips. Izzy was an exception to her 'I don't like animals' rule. That dog was a pure sweetheart. She was a Great Dane/Bloodhound mix and was so ugly, she was adorable. One ear stayed up, one flopped down. She had one white eye, one black eye. She was spotted almost like a Dalmatian. Izzy was one strange looking pooch.

Opening the door, she braced herself for Izzy's impact and wagged her finger to quiet her down. "You shush, missy. No howling." She looked up at Jody with humor in her eyes. "Hey Jody, thanks a lot for letting us borrow her. I think she's just what Crystal needs. Do you want to meet her?"

"Hell yes. I can't believe this. It's all so surprising. I can't imagine how Vlad's dealing with it."

"Well, he's a little lost right now. I guess we all are, but Crystal most of all. I think Izzy will help her get through her first night." Jody loved Izzy as much as he did his wife.

Jody bent down and unclipped Izzy's leash. She took off toward the sound of Vlad's voice, letting out a "woof, woof!" as she went. Running on the wood floors, she sounded more like a herd of elephants than a mere dog.

"Well, I guess she'll introduce herself," Jody said.

His words were no sooner out when they heard a squeal of delight. It was the first sound of happiness Zoe had heard

Crystal make, and it warmed her all the way to her toes. She looked up at Jody and said, "Thank you."

Vlad was caught by surprise when Izzy came flying into the room. She tried to stop in front of Crystal, but slid on the wood floors and took them both down into a heap of child and dog. Izzy was quick to roll off the little girl and start licking her face amid happy yelps.

"Izzy. What are you doing here, girl?" Vlad turned his head as he heard footsteps behind him. "Jody?"

Jody walked over to Vlad and quietly congratulated him. "She's a beauty."

"Thanks. It's pretty shocking, but we'll figure it out."

"Izzy's here for a sleepover. Zoe thought it might help your daughter sleep for a night or two." Jody smiled at the sight of Izzy and Crystal playing on the floor.

"Crystal?" Zoe walked over to get her attention. Crystal looked up at her with a joyful smile on her face.

"Did you see the dog run into me? She made me fall and then fell on top of me! She's funny." Crystal was so animated. She looked just like any other eight year old without a care in the world. Zoe knew a dog wasn't going to take away her pain overnight, but it would give her a source of joy in her daily life.

"I did. Her name's Izzy. She's our friends' dog and here for a sleepover if you want her to be." Zoe took her hand and helped her stand up. Izzy sat right beside her and was almost head-to-head with Crystal even though she was sitting. "This is Jody. He's a friend of your father's and Izzy's owner. He said she could sleep with you for a night or two if you want."

Crystal shyly looked up at Jody and said, "Thank you."

"You're welcome." Jody held his hand out to her, and she shook it. "It's nice to meet you, Crystal. Welcome to San Diego. Where did you used to live?"

Zoe held her breath. They hadn't really asked her any personal questions so far, and she wasn't sure how Crystal would react.

"My mom and I lived in Vancouver. She died, and now I have to live with him. I mean, my father." She looked sad, but Izzy licked her face and immediately took some of her sadness away.

"I'm sorry you lost your mom, but I'm glad you're here." Jody gave Izzy a pat on the head and told her to stay with Crystal. "Okay guys, well, I'm going to get going." He addressed Crystal again. "Just so you know, she's a bed hog, and she might try to pull your covers off."

Crystal smiled and looked at Izzy. "That's okay. She can have some of my covers."

Zoe tucked Crystal and Izzy into bed later that evening. She sat with Crystal, telling her stories of when she used to ride horses as a little girl, until she fell asleep. With a stern look at Izzy to stay, Zoe carefully got up off the bed to go talk to Vlad.

She found him in the living room, sitting on the couch, a glass of scotch in his hand. He didn't seem to be drinking it. It was more of a prop to give him something to hold on to.

"Is she asleep?" Vlad tried to put Crystal to bed, but she only wanted Zoe. She was still avoiding Vlad at all costs.

"Yeah." Zoe slid onto the couch and Vlad pulled her up against him, kissing her hair.

"I don't know what I would have done without you today, Zoe. I still can't wrap my mind around all of this. It must be so scary for her, coming to live with a father she never knew. It's hard to believe that she doesn't have any other family. Well, that she knew about."

"It is scary for her. I remember how it feels, Vlad. I only had my little brother after my parents died. Well, him and that nasty old bitch we had to live with until I was eighteen."

"You never did tell me the details of your life after your parents died. Care to share some with me now?"

Zoe sighed. "I just don't like to think about it. They weren't good years for us." Aside from seeing Aidan as often as both of their schedules allowed, Zoe didn't want any reminders of the time they had lived with her mother's great aunt, Sophie. She was a nasty woman.

"Well, do you think you would be able to talk to Crystal about it someday? Maybe it would help her. I know she wouldn't want to hear about it now, but maybe later. And then someday you'll trust me enough to share your secrets with me." Vlad felt bad that Zoe wasn't comfortable talking to him.

"It's not about trust, Vlad. It's just that the aunt who kept us for five years after our parents died was a terror. And I don't mean a terror as in she took our TV privilege away. I mean terror as in she locked Aidan in a tiny closet for a week, only letting him out four times a day for meals and bathroom breaks. All because he told her he thought he was gay."

Vlad kept silent and slowly stroked her back.

"One time, Aidan peed on the floor in there because she wouldn't let him out to go to the bathroom in the middle of the night. She made him scrub it up with his t-shirt and then made him wear that t-shirt to school for the next three days." Vlad could feel Zoe's body tensing up as she spoke. "I hated her for that. I worked every day after school to save money so that we could move as soon as I turned eighteen."

Vlad was speechless. He picked up her hand, squeezing it in comfort. "My God. That's a terrible thing for someone to do. How did you two get through that, Zoe?" He looked into her eyes in wonder. "To survive in that kind of environment—you're amazing."

She squeezed his hand back and gave him a sad smile. "That was just one of her many punishments for us. At least she's dead now. I think her main issue with us was that she couldn't get her hands on our trust funds. Dad left her enough to care for us—not that she used the money for that—but she couldn't ever touch our trust funds. I couldn't access mine until I was twenty-one. It's nice Aidan and I don't ever have to worry about money again, but it would have been better if Dad had known how evil Aunt Sophie was. If I could have gotten to my trust fund at eighteen, I could have done better with Aidan."

Vlad knew Zoe came from money. Lacey had mentioned something about Zoe spending her trust fund on furniture and things so that she could donate her old stuff. She would purposely buy new things every few years so that she could give her older stuff away. It mostly went to underprivileged people, but sometimes she gave stuff to nursing homes or even hospitals for their waiting rooms. She allowed people to feel as if they weren't taking charity since she was simply buying new things any way. That's just the kind of person she was.

"For what it's worth, I think you did a great job with Aidan. I don't know him all that well yet, but from what I've seen, he's a well-adjusted kid with a great sense of humor. And he's confident in his sexuality. You gave him that, Zoe. Being gay can't be easy."

Zoe smiled at that. "It doesn't hurt that he's gorgeous. He goes to school for architecture, and he winds up modeling all over the world. It's a good thing that Gary isn't the jealous type and likes to travel. Those two are so good together." Aidan had had so many bad relationships. He was too good and honest so he tended to get taken advantage of. That all stopped when he met Gary. Gary would slay anyone who tried to hurt Aidan.

"So, back to the subject we *should* be discussing. What are your plans for your daughter?"

"I don't know. I think I'd like to maybe buy a house, though. This isn't the right kind of place to raise a little girl. But then, what about us? I don't want to buy a house without you. We should get married first. But is that too much for Crystal? Should I live with her alone and get to know her first? Christ! I don't know what to do." Vlad didn't want to disappoint anyone, himself included.

"Vlad. I think we should put us on hold for now. Get to know your daughter. We can talk about us later."

Vlad's grip got uncomfortably tight on Zoe's waist as he was rubbing up and down her back. "What? No. No way, Zoe. You're not fucking this up now. We're getting married. Daughter or not, she's not going to interfere with our relationship. I waited for you for years, Zoe. Years."

"Whoa. Calm down. Vlad, I'm not going anywhere, I just think we should take a step back. Hell, I wasn't even sure if bringing Izzy here would be another big change for her. I'm not up on all of my child psychology. I deal with big kids, remember?" Zoe knew that Crystal needed to get a feeling of stability. A feeling of belonging. She wasn't sure if her newly-found father getting married would do that for her. She just didn't want to throw another wrench into the situation.

"Why don't we just get through the night and see what tomorrow brings, okay? I'm going to bed." Zoe tried to get up, but Vlad held her tight.

"Can you just sit here with me for a minute and let me hold you? I just need a couple of minutes of sanity. Please." Vlad tucked her head into his neck, put his drink on the table, and gathered her close in his arms. She gave him a sense of security, and he needed that for just a few minutes.

Chapter 17

Zoe awoke to the sounds of pans banging in the kitchen. She opened her eyes, surprised to see the bed empty. It had been a long night for her, with Izzy taking up half the bed and Crystal kicking her incessantly as she tossed from side to side.

"What's all this noise?" Zoe asked sleepily as she made her way into the kitchen, rubbing her eyes. The sight that greeted her was sweet but looked a little strained. She had to give them credit, though. They were both making an effort to get comfortable with one other.

Vlad whipped eggs together and cooked bacon as Crystal busied herself by feeding the dog.

"Good morning, Zoe. We're making you breakfast. It was Crystal's idea."

Crystal spared Zoe a quick look and nodded her head, before returning her full attention to Izzy's food bowl.

Vlad caught Zoe's eye and shook his head. "She still won't talk to me," he mouthed to her.

"Crystal, since the room you slept in last night will be yours, why don't you tell your father how you'd like to decorate it?" Zoe knew that Vlad had talked about moving into a house, but she thought Crystal might want to tell him about what she liked. It would be nice to find something that she was comfortable talking to Vlad about—anything would do.

"It's okay the way it is."

A blue room with dark curtains and a dark wood bed was not how a little girl's room should be decorated. "Don't you want to paint it a prettier color, Crystal?" Vlad asked.

She looked up at him before pretending to be busy picking up Izzy's bowl, which was now empty. "It doesn't matter. Can I go back there and read now?"

Vlad remembered to hold in his exasperated sigh at the last minute. "Sure, honey. I'll call you when breakfast is ready."

Without another word, she tapped Izzy on the head and waved her hand so the dog would follow her. When she was gone, Vlad handed Zoe a letter. "Here's one of the letters Carla left me."

"Are you sure you want me to read this, Vlad? I imagine it's pretty personal." She had to admit, she was curious as hell about the woman who had had Vlad's child. It was an awful thing to feel about a dead woman, but she was a tiny bit jealous of her.

"I don't want to keep anything from you, Zoe. You know I have a past. I knew her long before I ever met you. And I know you have a past, too."

"Okay, I'll read it."

Dear Vlad,

I'm sure that you're pretty upset with me right about now. I am truly sorry that I never told you about Crystal. I hope you won't hold that against her.

Those months that we dated were some of the happiest times of my life. You were everything everyone thought you were—honest, fun, loving, and faithful. Thank you for all of that. It's because of those things that I've kept our daughter from you.

I know you would have done the 'right thing' and married me. You would have forced me into marriage, because you would have believed it was the best thing for us. And we would have been miserable. I could never be a hockey wife, and you could never give up hockey for family life, especially when you were in the best playing shape of your life. And I was only twenty-three. I didn't want to be tied to one man for the rest of my life.

These reasons probably sound pretty weak. I can only say that I did give it significant thought and believed this was the best solution for all of us, Crystal included. I never would have wanted our daughter to feel like she was a second thought to you. Oh, I know you would have tried to be home and in her life as much as possible, but with your schedule, it just wouldn't have worked for me. I wanted it all: the adoring husband home for dinner every night, the white picket fence—all of it.

The ironic part is that I never got it anyway. I guess not too many men want to be saddled with a twenty-three year old single mother. I may have been better off staying with you, but we'll never know, so it doesn't rate thinking about.

I ask that you give Crystal a place in your heart. I gave her your name so that she might find you someday when she was ready. I thought I'd have time to explain things when she got older, but I don't.

Please forgive me. I didn't keep her from you out of spite or anger or anything else. I only did what I thought was best.

There's one more thing I want you to know. I named her Crystal because it made me think about the way the ice in the rink would shine when it was fresh—before any skates marred the surface. And that made me think of you. I did care for you, very much.

Love her, Vlad. Open your heart and your home to her. Please. Give her all the love I won't be able to. She is the best little girl you'll ever know. She's worth any sacrifice you may have to make. I swear it.

Carla

Zoe looked up at Vlad after reading the letter, her eyes bright with unshed tears. "Wow. Hard to hold a grudge after reading that, isn't it? I can't help but feel for her. I still don't think there's any excuse for not telling someone they have a child, but I understand a little better why she felt she needed to keep Crystal to herself. How did the letter make you feel?" Zoe cringed at her choice of words. Vlad *hated* when she went into 'therapist mode' with him.

He raised his eyebrow, but let it go. "I feel the same way you do. I can't say I'm not mad, but who am I to say how I would have reacted back then? I just don't know, and it really doesn't matter now, does it?"

"No, it really doesn't." Zoe wasn't sure how Vlad would take her next suggestion. "Vlad, I think I'm going to go home after breakfast. I'll drop dopey dog off at Lacey's on my way. Why don't you and Crystal go do something together without me? I'll entertain your family for the day, and we can meet back at my house this afternoon. We can order pizza or something."

Vlad looked panicked. His eyes were darting around the room, and he fidgeted with the pan of eggs on the stove. "Uh, like what? What should we do?"

Zoe wanted to help him, she did, but she knew he had to figure some of it out on his own. "I don't know. Maybe take her to the beach? You need to try to break down that wall she has around you. Just do it gently. Remember that she's young and hurting and doesn't know what to do with it."

"Fuck, Zoe. I don't know what to do with it either!"

"I know, but you're the adult. You have to have patience with her."

"Yeah, okay." He didn't feel like talking about it anymore. "Eggs are ready."

"I'll go get Crystal."

Zoe found her on the bed reading *Green Eggs and Ham* by Dr. Seuss. "There won't be any green eggs at the table today," Zoe said with a smile. "But breakfast is ready."

After they ate, Zoe told Crystal that she was going to take Izzy home and that she'd see them later. "You two can come to my house this afternoon and stay for dinner. How does that sound?"

"Do you have any animals?" Crystal asked.

"No, I don't. But we can take a walk after dinner to get ice cream."

"Okay."

Vlad took Crystal to the store to buy a kite. She picked out Hello Kitty, and they drove to the beach. She still only gave one-word answers to direct questions he asked, and this point, he'd do just about anything if she would open up to him.

"Do you know how to fly a kite, Crystal?"

"No."

Vlad took a breath. He knew that she was only trying to cope as best she knew how, but his frustration was mounting.

"Well, me neither. We'll have to learn together, okay?" He didn't expect an acknowledgment and didn't get one. He read the directions, put the kite together, and got it in the air. Finally, she looked interested.

"Do you want to hold it?"

"Yes! Please."

As soon as he gave it to her, her face lit up. For the first time since she showed up on his doorstep, he felt like a father. "That's it. Good job, Little Bit!"

She faltered at the sound of the nickname Vlad had given her and let go of the kite. Vlad tried to grab it, but it went sailing away. Crystal looked at him, lip trembling.

He opened his arms to her, and to his ultimate surprise, she launched herself into them. "Oh, it's okay, sweetheart. I know you didn't mean to let it go. We'll get another one."

Through her hiccupping cries, he heard her say, "Why does everything go away?"

He thought of a million things he could say, but none that would make any difference. It obviously wasn't the kite she was crying over. He settled on the truth. "I don't know, little bit, sometimes they just do." He continued to hold her until her hiccups subsided, and she became her normal stoic self.

She pushed away from him, wiping her eyes with her sleeve. "Sorry."

Sad that she had put her walls back up, he took her hand and led her to the car. "Should we go get another kite, or do you want to go to Zoe's now?"

"Zoe's, please."

It was a silent drive, but when they walked into Zoe's house, Crystal's eyes lit up. It was clear that she felt more comfortable at Zoe's. He understood. He was a guy, and his place was a bachelor's pad, while Zoe's place was homey. What little girl, especially one who had just lost her mother, wouldn't want a cozy, happy home to stay in?

Vlad walked up to her and kissed her on the cheek. "Hi, Zoe."

"Hi to you, too." She walked over to Crystal and, very casually, gave her a kiss on the cheek. "How was your day? Did you and your father have fun?"

"I lost our kite." She burst into tears and hugged Zoe around the waist. She held on so tight, Zoe had to struggle not to push her away to take a breath.

Over Crystal's head, she looked at Vlad with questioning eyes. His face reflected his shock at Crystal's outburst. He apparently thought she was all cried out. Zoe gently but firmly turned the girl into Vlad's arms.

He picked her up and held her tight. Stroking her hair, he crooned in her ear, "Shhh, it's okay, little bit. It's okay." He simply let her cry and felt something soften inside him when he felt her little arms squeeze him tight. That was his daughter clutching him for comfort. He'd never felt so big. He felt like he could rope the moon! He kissed her cheek and put her down, kneeling before her.

"We'll get another kite if you want, and I'll tie it to your wrist so it doesn't go away ever again, okay?" He knew replacing the lost kite wasn't the cure all, but felt it was important to give her the option of replacing it.

She sniffled and wiped her nose on her sleeve. "Okay."

Apparently their moment was over as she looked at Zoe. "I'm hungry."

Dinner was a lively affair. Vlad's family was at the beach when he and Crystal had arrived. Shortly before dinner, they bounded noisily into the house talking about the warm sixty-degree weather. The temperature in Ukraine that time of year hovered around forty.

After devouring two slices of pizza each and some cheese fries, Crystal and the triplets fell asleep on the couch watching *The Lion King*.

Vlad and Zoe had some time to themselves as they did the dishes. The rest of his family was busy packing for their early morning flight. "So, how was your day? Was it awful when Crystal lost the kite?"

"Well, I know this sounds really bad, but I was glad it happened. She ran to me, Zoe. She actually ran to me. Granted, she burst into tears, but she ran to me for comfort. Hell. She's going to have me wrapped around her little finger in no time at all. I don't think there's anything I wouldn't do for her. We briefly talked about my buying her a pony. A pony, for Christ's sake!" He tried to act outraged, but his sappy smile gave him away.

"Sounds like progress. Vlad, things like that are going to affect her more than they would another child for quite a while. We see it as having to buy another kite. She sees it as something that left her and can't be replaced. She understands that you didn't know about her in her head, but her heart most likely feels like you abandoned her. It's going to take time, but it sounds like you had a good day. She certainly doesn't seem as leery of you today."

"No, she's not. She'd still prefer you, I think, but it's progress. She mentioned wanting to stay here tonight. Do you think it would be the wrong thing to do if I told her no? I don't want her to think of you as the good guy and me as the one she's stuck with." *Shit, that didn't sound right.* "No, wait. I didn't mean that I don't want her to love you, of course I do ..."

Zoe raised her hand to stop him. "Vlad, *please,* don't think about us right now. I get it. Concentrate on your daughter. I'll tell her that I have to leave on business or something, and she can't stay tonight. But, so she knows I'm not leaving her, are you okay with my telling her that she can stay another time?"

When Zoe had raised her hand up to him, he realized that he still hadn't placed a ring on her finger. He wanted to rectify that as soon as possible. Maybe that was something he and Crystal could do together. Girls liked jewelry. "Absolutely. Thanks again, Zoe. I love you. Have I told you that today?" Crystal walked in on them kissing.

"Ew, yuck." She walked right back out again, shaking her head in disgust.

Zoe and Vlad burst out laughing. "Well, that was a typical eight-year-old reaction." Vlad followed Crystal back into the living room to see what she needed.

"Where are the girls?"

"They got called upstairs to pack their things."

Vlad waited for her to tell him what she wanted, but she stayed quiet. "What did you want when you came into the kitchen, honey?"

She looked up at him with those cornflower blue eyes that looked so like his mother's, but didn't answer him. He didn't get it. One minute she was hugging him, and the next, she wouldn't even answer a direct question.

"Well? Did you need me?"

"No."

Vlad clenched his teeth, searching for patience. "Did you need Zoe?"

"No."

"Crystal, you must have needed something. What is it?"

"Nothing."

"Okay. I give up." Vlad threw up his hands and stormed out of the room. He passed Zoe on his way out and continued walking right out the door until he was standing on the deck listening to the sound of the waves crashing against the shoreline.

A couple of minutes passed before the door opened, and Vlad turned to see his mother standing there. "Did you lose your patience, Vladimir?"

"Yes, Mother, I did. I don't know what the hell she wants from me. I don't know what to do, and when I ask her, she doesn't answer me. God, am I an idiot for thinking I can be a father to her? I don't even know how to break through to her."

Emma started laughing. She was actually laughing at him! "I don't find this even remotely fucking funny, Mother."

She tried to erase her smile, but he could still see it tugging at her lips. "Of course not, dear, but watch your language. You don't want your daughter to hear you talking like that. And your father would backhand you. Are you done now?"

She could always make him feel so small. Rolling his eyes at himself more than her, he said, "Yes, I'm done."

"Good. Now, let's see if we can think this through. Your daughter lost her mother and came to live with a father she never knew existed. It's her first holiday alone. She's only been here for one day and one night. Let me say that again. *One* day and *one* night. And in that short amount of time, she has actually turned to you twice."

"Yeah, I know you're right. But why the hell won't she answer me when I ask her a question? I'll bet she'll talk to Zoe. Seems she'll always talk to Zoe." Apparently he was mad at Zoe now?

Emma gave him an indulgent smile. "Vlad, she's a little girl. She lost her *mother.* I think it's very natural that she would gravitate toward Zoe. Good thing she's your girlfriend, isn't it?"

"That's another thing. She's not just my girlfriend. She asked me to marry her. We were going to tell you all at brunch this morning."

"*She* asked *you?* Oh, Vlad, that's wonderful!" She leaned over and hugged him. "We love her. She's perfect for you, you know." He could tell his mother was a bit confused though. "If you're so in love with this woman, why are you mad that Crystal likes her? I'm not understanding this, Vladimir."

"Because. She's *my* daughter, not Zoe's. Her mother already kept her away from me. I'm not going to let Zoe swoop in and be the parent. I've lost enough time with her!" Jesus, he sounded like an idiot. He knew he did.

"You need to talk to Zoe. It seemed to me that you were more than happy to have her help earlier, but now you don't want it. You can't be mad at her for doing what you asked. We all saw the helpless way you looked at her when Crystal first showed up."

"Hell, I know that, Mom." He shrugged his shoulders as he walked over and gripped the railing, staring out into the night. "I guess I'm jealous. It's like there's a girls' club and boys aren't allowed. I want her to come to *me*. I want her to want to be in *my* club."

Emma put her arm around her son and stood at the railing with him. "She will, sweetie, but you have to give her time. And you need to dig deep and be more patient with her. You're an adult. We can process things quicker than children. It's only been a day, Vlad. One day."

Vlad bowed his head and reached up to cover his mother's hand with his own. "Thanks, Mom. I'll try harder. I want her to feel safe and happy. Of course patience has never been my strong suit, and obviously you need a lot to be a parent."

"I know you will. And yes, you absolutely do." She patted his arm and left him to gather his thoughts.

Vlad and Crystal did wind up spending the night at Zoe's. Crystal asked him if she could, and he simply said yes. He knew he'd have to work on saying no to her someday, but today wasn't that day.

Vlad's parents had left to go back to his place to spend the night, taking Ruslan and Anna with them. The triplets stayed to be with Crystal as long as they could. Sipping coffee in the kitchen, Zoe asked, "So, where are you going to sleep, Vlad?"

She wasn't worried about what Crystal would think if they slept in the same bed. She knew a lot of people would frown on that, but they shouldn't be concerned about other people anyway. She and Vlad were in a committed relationship and had plans to marry, but she'd leave it up to him.

"Next to you, if you let me. Hell, we're going to be married soon. Is it that big of a deal?"

Zoe smiled. "No, I don't think it is. But there won't be any sex tonight. We have to be available for Crystal. She can sleep in with the other kids. We can make a fort for them or something so they can all sleep on the floor together."

"Sounds like a plan. But why no sex?" Of course that was the first thing Vlad thought about when she said he could sleep in her bed. "I'll be quiet. *You're* the loud one anyway."

"So? You like me loud." She knew he'd agree. She wasn't disappointed.

"Yes, ma'am, I do."

Zoe laughed as she pushed him away when he advanced on her, a lecherous look in his eyes. "You need to be aware if your daughter needs you. She'll probably be fine being with the girls, but you never know. She needs all of your attention for a while."

Vlad wasn't happy, but he relented. "Fine. No sex."

Chapter 18

After a night spent tossing and turning, Vlad felt like he'd been run over by a Mack truck. He resisted the urge to check on Crystal a dozen times during the night, but only because Zoe flung her leg over him and reassured him that Crystal would come to them if she needed too. But as soon as he heard sounds coming from the girls' room, he was up and knocking on their door.

"Girls? You awake?" He heard lots of giggling and mumbling. He assumed that meant yes. "Get up and get dressed. You only have a couple of hours before you have to be at the airport. Come downstairs for breakfast when you're done."

He really wanted to peek in at his daughter, but Zoe convinced him otherwise. Girls needed their privacy, even at that age, she told him.

Vlad was in the kitchen, fresh from the shower, when the girls came running in. "We're starving, Vlad! What's for breakfast?"

"Let's see. I have eggs, bacon and toast—hmmm, we just need something sweet." He looked around the kitchen with a devilish look. He slowly moved toward the girls, and the triplets backed up a step. They knew that game.

Lena spoke up first. "Oh, no. Not the tickle monster!" She looked at her sisters and Crystal. "Run!"

The girls took off into the living room, screeching in joy as Vlad chased them. He caught Sasha first and threw her on the couch, tickling her mercilessly. She squealed in delight. When he felt a pillow slammed into his head, he turned and grabbed the culprit, but in doing so, he lost his hold on Sasha.

In no time at all, he found himself pinned down by the girls as they tickled him. He laughed until his sides hurt. "Okay, uncle. I cry uncle!" He looked up to see Zoe watching them. Crystal was just about to hit him with the pillow again when he pleaded for help. "Help me, Zoe. These girls are too strong."

Zoe walked over and sat down next to Vlad. "Okay girls, I'm here to help." She pinned Vlad's arms down and let the girls tickle him until he had tears in his eyes from laughing so hard.

He was just wriggling around to get up when Crystal fell and landed on his hip. "Fuck!"

Zoe immediately let go of his hands and picked Crystal up to get her off him. Vlad rolled over to try and mask the pain radiating from his hip.

"Oh my God. I'm sorry. I'm sorry." Crystal stared at him in absolute horror. She'd obviously not meant to hurt him.

She walked over to Vlad, who was just starting to get up and held her hand out to him. "I'm sorry. I'll help you up. I didn't mean to hurt you."

"I know you didn't, sweetheart. I'm sorry I yelled like that. And such a bad word. I had surgery on that hip a while ago, and you just hit a bad spot, that's all. I'll be fine." It was starting to feel better already. He was afraid that he might have damaged something, though.

Just as it looked like she might burst into tears, which he didn't think he could stand, the doorbell rang. "That must be your grandparents. You want to go get the door for me?"

Crystal looked around and saw everyone looking at her. "Okay." Her footsteps could be heard all the way to the front door as she ran to answer it. The triplets quickly followed her.

Vlad looked at Zoe. "Fucked up again, didn't I?"

"Nah. One bad word isn't going to ruin her for life, but really, you should try to take that out of your vocabulary. At least when you're around children. Are you really okay now?"

He stood up and took a couple of steps. He could feel a twinge of pain, but it was okay. "I think so. I'll call the doctor tomorrow just to make sure."

When everyone had left to go to the airport, Crystal lost some of her bravado. She seemed to be more comfortable when there were more people around.

The couch in the living room was still a mess from their playtime earlier. Crystal was just putting the cushions back in place when he walked in.

"Hey, Little Bit. I need your help." He looked around to make sure Zoe was still upstairs in the shower, out of hearing distance. "You know Zoe and I are getting married, but I didn't buy a ring for her yet."

She interrupted him. "You didn't buy her a ring? You're supposed to have the ring when you ask her to marry you. That's how the princes do it."

Vlad gave a short laugh and a smile. "You're right, of course, but Zoe asked *me* to marry *her*. I still want to buy her a ring. She has work to do today, so how about if we go shopping, and you can help me pick one out? Would you do that?"

"I like jewelry, so yes, I'll help you."

The mall was huge. It was a sprawling building with stores and restaurants intermixed. Right in the middle was a burger joint that housed an arcade and an indoor mini golf course.

When Crystal saw the giant dinosaur standing next to the mini golf sign, she gasped. "I love dinosaurs," she whispered reverently.

"Do you? Would you like to play mini golf before we buy Zoe's ring?"

"No, that's okay." She looked back down into her lap, like she had said something wrong.

Vlad pressed his lips together, fighting for patience. "Look, Crystal. I know this is all hard for you. I know you'd rather not be here with me, but I'd like to do things with you. And I want you to tell me what you like to do. I want to know about the things you like and don't like. So, I say we go play mini golf. There's only one thing I need you to do for me."

She looked up at him when he didn't say any more. "What do you need me to do?"

He patted his right side. "Well, this hip is still a little sore. Would you pick up my golf ball for me? I don't think it's good for me to bend like that a lot right now."

She smiled shyly at him. "I can do that for you." She seemed to like the fact that he needed her help.

"Good, let's go."

The dinosaurs inside the mall were huge. There were quite a few types placed strategically next to potted plants and even some trees. Vlad could certainly see why so many people enjoyed going there. He was not a shopper himself, but he had to admit, the place had everything.

After dodging T-Rex legs and a flying Pterodactyl who simply did not want to let his ball through, he gave up all pretense of being good at golf. His hockey buddies would have a field day with him. Hockey players were supposed to be good at golf. It was, after all, their summer sport. Most of the guys held golf tournaments for charity in the off season. He secretly hated the game, but he enjoyed seeing Crystal's concentration as she tried to dodge the closing legs and flapping wings.

When her ball hit Rex's leg for the third time, she sighed like a grown up and placed her hand on her forehead in disgust. "I can't do this, Dad. It's too hard."

Vlad instantly felt a burning pressure in his eyes. She'd called him Dad like it was a normal occurrence. He wanted to pick her up, swing her around, and hold her tight, but he was

166

learning and knew that would make her uncomfortable, so he didn't say anything about it.

"Don't look at me. I can't do it either. Rex has my number for sure." Vlad looked around and rubbed his chin. "I have an idea. How about if we try it together?" He'd get that damn ball through if it killed him!

"How?"

Vlad walked over and stood over her so that they could grip the golf club together. "I'm not sure. Maybe like this? I know. Let's line it up, and then close our eyes and just go for it."

She looked up at him, doubt in her eyes. "Okay, but I don't think it's going to work." They did as he said.

"Okay. No peeking. Ready? One ... two ... three!" They whacked the ball and heard a solid *thunk* as it hit Rex's leg. "Dammit," he mumbled.

Crystal laughed. "We're not very good at this, are we?"

He looked into her eyes and smiled. "I think we're doing okay, Little Bit. I think we're doing just fine."

It was like someone flipped a switch. He felt her body stiffen, and she stepped out of his arms. "Let's just go get Zoe's ring, can we?" He thought he saw her lip trembling.

There was no one else in their general area and he carefully got down on his knee. "What's wrong, Crystal? We were having fun. Honey, what happened?"

He could tell she was fighting so hard to be happy, but it just didn't work all the time. He saw a tear escape and resisted the urge to pull her to him. In that tiny voice she used, she told him what she was feeling. "It's just that when I start to feel happy, I feel sad. My mom is dead. Why should I feel happy?" She clenched her little hands as another tear escaped.

"Ah, honey. It's okay." Zoe had told him to let her feel what she was feeling and to accept it. She told him to let Crystal know that he was okay with her being sad. "You're going to feel sad a lot for a while. That's okay. Your mom was a wonderful mother."

"How do you know?"

"Because I know you. Your mother did a great job with you. You're a fabulous little girl, and that's because of how your mom raised you. I'll tell you something else. She'd want you to be happy. If you think about it, you know it's true. Just because you feel happy doesn't mean you don't miss your mother."

Crystal listened to what he said. "So Mommy would be mad at me for being sad?"

"No!" *Christ! Was he fucking this up, too?* "No, honey, not at all. Nothing that you feel is wrong. It's okay to feel sad, but it's also okay to feel happy. Your mom would understand the sadness and be proud of how much you love her, but she would also want you to find happiness and live a wonderful life."

She sniffled, but seemed to accept that. "Okay. Should we finish the game then?"

"Do you want to? If we do, can we just move onto the next hole? This T-Rex is killing me."

She smiled slightly and picked up their golf balls. "Yeah, let's go to the next one. I think it's just one of those big leaf eater guys."

They eventually made it to the eighteenth hole. There was only one other hole they couldn't get through with a very stubborn Triceratops.

"We did okay for a couple of newbie dinosaur mini golfers, don't you think?" Vlad was happy about their day so far.

"Well, we had to cheat a little, but I won't tell if you don't." She gifted him with one of her rare smiles that lit up her face.

Vlad made the motion of zipping his lips. "Not a word." They were walking through the mall when he smelled burgers and his stomach grumbled. "You hungry?"

"I could eat a dinosaur!" She laughed at her own joke.

"Well, how about a burger instead?"

While they were eating their burgers, Vlad started to gently inquire about her life at home. "Do you want to tell me about things you liked to do back home?" He hated to use the word 'home', as San Diego was her home now, but maybe that would be more comfortable for her at the moment.

"I played soccer. I really like that." She smiled and looked up at him quickly before giving her attention back to her cheeseburger. "I'm a goalie."

Vlad's eyes widened. He didn't see any record of that in Carla's notes that she left him. "Really? That's great, Crystal. Would you like to play here? We can look into it. I have to register you for school anyway. We need to go there tomorrow, so you can start next week." He held his breath for her reaction.

"I don't want to go to school, but I know I have to. Yes, I do want to play soccer, if that's okay?"

He hated the way she asked if everything was okay. Most kids would demand to be allowed to play. He didn't agree with the way some kids ruled their parents, but he didn't want her to be afraid to ask for things either. He also understood that most kids didn't lose their mothers to cancer and get uprooted to live with a father they never knew they had.

"I know it's going to be hard to start a new school, but maybe if you join the school's soccer team, you'll make new friends even quicker. Speaking of friends, if you have some you'd like to call, you can. Anytime."

"Really? I haven't talked to my friend Emmy in a week! I miss her."

"Of course. You can call her everyday if you want. And she can come visit if her parents say it's okay." Vlad wanted to make her adjustment as easy as possible.

"Thank you."

"You're welcome. Now, if you're done, let's go buy Zoe a ring."

They didn't immediately go back to Zoe's when they were done at the mall. They took a detour to a furniture store so Crystal could pick out new bedroom furniture.

"What are we doing here?"

"I want you to pick out a new bedroom set. You don't want that furniture that's in there now, I know it." Vlad spread his hands wide over the showroom. "Pick out anything you want."

Her eyes lit up as she took in the store. "Really? Anything I want? Wow, we had all used stuff at home."

Vlad winced when he heard that. He could have bought them anything they needed all those years. What good was all the money he had if he didn't know Carla could have used it to raise his daughter. It was so frustrating. "Really. Anything you want. Bed, bureau, lamps, anything."

She made a bee line over to a pink canopy bed. The frame was whitewashed oak with a soft pink, lacy canopy. It was covered with a big, fluffy white comforter that had pink flowers embroidered around the edges. Four pillows, the size of Crystal, adorned the head of the bed, while one long, pink bolster pillow sat at the foot. "This is pretty. So pretty."

"Do you want to look around some more? This is the first bed you've seen."

"No, thank you. I like this one. Is that okay? The pillows are so pretty."

The salesman had walked over and heard her comment. "I'm sorry, the coverings and pillows are just for show."

Vlad looked up at him and pulled out his wallet. "I'm sure we could work something out."

As soon as the salesman looked at Vlad, recognition kicked in. "Vlad Bejsiuk! I'm a big fan." He stuck out his hand and pumped Vlad's enthusiastically. "Of course we can work something out. Is there anything else I can show you?"

"For now, we'll take the whole bedroom set. Taking some big bills out of his wallet, he asked, "Is it possible to have this delivered today?" At the salesman's dubious look, Vlad pulled out a couple of more bills.

"Of course," he stammered.

Vlad was having fun. He never used his status or money to get things done. Well, okay, maybe he'd gotten a table at a crowded restaurant once or twice, but he never bullied with it. He hated people like that, but when it came to Crystal, he found it didn't bother him so much.

"We'll just take a look around and make sure there's nothing else we want, okay?"

"Absolutely. Let me just go and start making arrangements for delivery. If I could have your address?"

Vlad gave him the address and the phone number of the loading dock manager to his building. Deliveries of that size all came through the back and up the freight elevator. He then took Crystal's hand. "Let's go look at some lamps for your room."

After another hour in the store, Crystal had picked out a giraffe floor lamp, an elephant table lamp and a dainty pink and white desk where she could do her homework. The lamps didn't match by any stretch of the imagination, but Vlad didn't care at all. She enjoyed picking out her new furniture. And he enjoyed seeing her enjoy something.

She enjoyed it so much she actually asked Vlad if they could go shopping for new school clothes.

Vlad couldn't quite hold in his groan. He had had enough shopping for one day. Or month. "I'll be happy to buy you new clothes, Crystal, but how about if we see if Zoe will take you? She'd be much better at that than I would."

"Okay," she replied happily.

Chapter 19

Vlad was just moving the last piece of his furniture out of Crystal's room when the phone rang. "Hello?"

"Hi, Mr. Bejsiuk. This is Cal, from the loading dock. Your furniture is here, sir. Can we send it up now?"

"Sure, thanks."

After all of the furniture was moved in, and they were about to leave, Vlad caught one of the delivery guys eyeing the furniture that he'd just moved out of Crystal's room.

"You like it?"

The guy looked embarrassed to be caught ogling Vlad's stuff. "Sorry, sir. It just caught my eye. It looks like the same furniture my brother had. His house burned down about three months ago."

"That's rough. I'm sorry to hear that."

"Thanks. He'll be fine. We always are."

"Why don't you take it? Give it to him if you think he'd want it." Vlad was going to donate it anyway. It would be nice to be able to give it to someone who really needed it.

The guy's eyes widened in surprise, and he took half a step back. "What? Oh no, I couldn't, but thank you. He won't take charity. Even from you."

"What do you mean, 'even from me'?"

"Oh, he's a huge hockey fan. He's gonna die when I tell him I was here today."

Vlad smiled in appreciation. "That's great. The fact that he's a fan makes it even better. Come on, take it. I'm giving it away anyway. You're saving me the hassle of having to hire someone to haul it out of here. As long as he needs it, I'm happy to give it."

"You're really serious? Aw, man. This is great. His birthday is next weekend. He'll flip!" He hesitated as he started to walk toward the bed frame. "Could I snap a picture of you in front of the furniture with my phone? You know, so people believe him?"

"Sure, what the hell." Vlad let the kid take the picture and gave him a signed puck to take with him, too.

"Thanks, man. You have no idea how much this will mean to him. He's had a rough couple of months. I hope your hip's feeling better."

"Thanks. It's getting better every day." The kid nodded at him and then got busy carrying out Vlad's old furniture.

After the delivery guys left, it was time for dinner. It was a little awkward, eating alone with Crystal in his place, but not as bad as the other times they were without Zoe and other people around.

"Do you want to watch TV while I clean up in here, Crystal?"

"No. That's okay." She continued to simply sit at the table watching him.

"Do you want to call your friend?"

"It's Sunday, and she's with her father this weekend. Her parents are divorced."

Shit. What am I supposed to do with her? "Um, what do you want to do?"

"Is it okay if I take the hockey blanket from the couch and sit on the patio to play?"

"Sure. Maybe I'll bring you some hot chocolate when I'm done here."

She got up and moved toward the living room to grab the blanket. "Okay."

Vlad made a quick phone call to Zoe as soon as Crystal walked outside. "Hey, gorgeous."

"Hi." Zoe was out of breath. "How was your day?"

"Been running, have you?" Vlad could just picture her standing in the kitchen, drinking a glass of water as sweat glistened over her. If he closed his eyes, he could visualize a tiny bead of moisture running down her neck, disappearing into her sports bra—simply sliding down to the Promised Land.

"Vlad? Are you there?"

He cleared his throat and snapped his eyes open, trying in vain to refocus his thoughts. "Oh—yeah."

Zoe laughed, obviously knowing exactly where Vlad's thoughts had gone. "You're thinking about me naked, aren't you?"

"Sort of. What are you wearing? Sports bra? Those tight running shorts?" He reached down to adjust himself so that he was more comfortable.

"Not anymore. I'm getting ready to hop in the shower. I have nothing on. Nothing. And I'm a little chilly. You know what that means. Hard … as … diamonds." Zoe loved to torture Vlad.

"Jesus, Zoe. Do you have to say things like that when I have an eight year old sitting out on the patio? I'm getting hard … as … diamonds, too, thank you."

"So you wouldn't want me to say, touch myself, right? Just slide my hand down over my breasts?" Zoe let out a low moan. "Slide them down until I can rub myself while I think about you fucking me?"

"Zoe! What's gotten into you tonight?" Vlad liked where her thoughts were, but not that he couldn't do anything to ease them both.

"I don't know. I am just really, really horny. God, I hate that word, but I am."

Vlad heard the hitch in her voice. "You're still touching yourself, aren't you?"

"Mmm hmm. I can't help it—feels so good."

Vlad sneaked a peek behind him to make sure Crystal was still content on the patio. She'd taken a couple of dolls out with her and was playing with them on the lounge chair.

"Fuck me, I wish I was there. You know what I would do to you?"

"No. Tell me. In vivid detail."

"I wouldn't let you touch yourself."

Zoe gasped. "That's not fun, Vlad. That's mean."

"Shhh. Shut up and listen. This is what I'd do. I'd take your hands and tie them behind your back. I'd strip off my clothes and put us both in the shower." He closed his eyes again so that he'd have a better picture of her in his mind.

In a voice, husky with pent up desire, Zoe asked, "Then what?"

"I'd kiss you, very slowly. Light kisses, teasing kisses. You'd try to lick my lips, and I'd pull back. This is my show. Then I'd lather up my hands with soap and rub them up and down your gorgeous body. Every inch of you. My hands would be soft in some places and rough in others. Can you feel it, Zoe?"

"God, yes. More, Vlad. I'm close."

"Oh no, Zoe. Not yet." At that moment, he opened his eyes, turning his head toward the door. Crystal was looking at him. He smiled at her and mimicked making her hot chocolate. She nodded her head and went back to playing with her dolls.

"Okay, I'm short on time here, so I'll let you keep touching yourself. I want you to pretend I'm kneeling between your legs. I know how much you like that."

"I do. God, I do."

"I'm going to lick you gently until you beg me for more. You'll beg me to let you come, Zoe. The first time you beg me, I'm going to pull back. Just when you try to grab me and pull me back, I'll bury my fingers into your bottom and pull you to me fast, sucking you hard. I want you to shatter into a million pieces."

"Yes!" He could hear Zoe panting and knew he'd taken her over the edge. "Oh, God! So good." He waited until her breathing became more regular and chuckled. It was a forced chuckle, as his jeans had become uncomfortably tight.

"This wasn't what I called for, you know? I'm hard as a fucking rock, and you're a pile of nicely sated bones. Not quite fair."

He could hear the smile in her voice. "Ah, Vlad. How many times have I told you? Life isn't always fair. I can't think now. Why don't you call me after Crystal is in bed and tell me how your day went? I need to shower, as soon as I can get up off the floor."

"You're welcome." He said sarcastically, shaking his head. "I love you, Zoe. Talk to you soon."

Chuckling she told him she loved him too. "Bye."

After Crystal had her hot chocolate and they played a few games of Candy Land, she started falling asleep. He gently picked her up and carried her to her room. She stirred slightly and looked up at him with fear in her eyes until she realized where she was.

"I'm awake. I need to brush my teeth and put my pajamas on."

Right. Of course she did. "Do you need any help?"

She looked at him like he had two heads. "No. I can do it myself." He turned away, and she stopped him. "Um, do you think you could come back when I'm done and read to me for a minute? You don't have to if you don't want to."

Vlad's chest tightened again in that way it had when she first called him Dad. "I'd love to read to you, Little Bit. Just give me a holler when you're ready."

"Okay."

Vlad read to Crystal for all of about five minutes before she was asleep. It had been a big day for both of them.

As he left her room, he turned on the overhead nightlight in her bathroom and left the door open a crack.

He went into his own room to watch TV until he fell asleep. At around half past two in the morning, Vlad heard Crystal scream. He ran into her room and found her awake, hitting herself.

"What are you doing, Crystal? Stop hitting yourself!" When Vlad grabbed her arms, she went ballistic.

"Stop! I know I'm still dreaming. You don't control me! Stop! Stop! Stop! You killed her! I saw you. I hate you. *I hate you!*" She tried to hit him, but he didn't let go of her arms.

He didn't know what to do. "Crystal, honey, wake up! Honey, wake up." She looked like she was still asleep. She was sitting up and talking, but her eyes were glazed over. She finally started to cry and launched herself into his arms.

"Am I really awake this time? Please, Daddy, am I really awake?"

He stroked her back, at a loss for words. That was the second time she called him Dad. "Yes, Little Bit, you're awake. I promise." He pulled her away and made her look at him. "See? I'm right here." Her breathing began to settle, and her tears subsided.

"I'm sorry I said I hate you. I don't."

"It's okay. Tell me what you were dreaming about."

"I'm not sure. It's hard to explain. I mean, the dream was just a dream, but I feel like I'm awake. And I think that I'm awake, but then I know I'm not because something awful happens, and I can't wake up. So I try hitting myself to wake up." She started crying again, and Vlad carried her into his room.

"Shhh. I'm here, Crystal. You can sleep with me tonight, okay?"

She didn't even answer him as she burrowed down beside him. He felt like Superman. His child was looking to him for protection, and it was humbling. "That's it, sweetheart, you go to sleep. I'll keep the monsters away."

The next night brought the same night terrors, as he found out they were called. They had only seen Zoe for lunch that day, but Vlad was able to get a couple of minutes alone with her. And they weren't good minutes.

"Oh, Vlad. Night terrors are scary. They don't usually last too long, maybe a week or two, but they're pretty terrible. It's not surprising that she's having them, you know. There's really nothing you can do other than be there for her, like you are." Zoe had also had night terrors after her mother died. "I'll talk to her if you want."

Vlad wasn't surprised that Crystal was having bad dreams either. It didn't take a PhD to understand it, either. He decided he didn't want Zoe to talk to her. It was sick, but he wanted

Crystal all to himself, even though he wanted to be a family with the three of them. It made no logical sense. After all, he did ask her before to talk to Crystal about her own parents dying.

"No. I'll take care of it." His voice was edged with silent animosity, unrealistic as it was.

"I'm only trying to help you, Vlad. What's wrong?"

"Look. I know you want to help, and you have all those fancy letters after your name, but I'm not stupid. She's *my* kid, and I'll take care of her. She needs to depend on *me*."

Zoe didn't take well to Vlad's attitude. "Well fuck you, Vlad! I know she's *your* kid. You remind me of that all the time. Jesus. It's not a competition. I just want to help her. You have no idea what she's going through. None! I do."

"Yeah. I know. The poor orphan Zoe with the trust fund. You've told me—several times. I get it. You had a terrible childhood. Well, she's still *my* child. *Mine!*" He had no idea why he was so mad, but he did know that it wasn't Zoe's fault.

Zoe took a step back, looking at him as if she didn't even recognize him. "Wow. Okay, get out. Just go." She loved him and only wanted to help; yet he just threw her childhood situation in her face. That was *not* okay.

"No. Wait. I didn't mean that, Zoe. You know I didn't." He took a step toward her, but she held him off.

"Just go, Vlad. You're right. You have Crystal now."

"No—Zoe, what are you saying? No. Look, I fucked up again. I do that. You know I do. Don't throw me out. I didn't mean any of it. I just—Fuck! I don't know, I don't know." He threw his hands up in surrender. How did things go so wrong so quickly?

Crystal walked back in from the living room where she had been watching TV. "Are you mad at me? I'm sorry."

Zoe could have kicked herself for letting Crystal hear them argue. "No, sweetie. Of course not. Your dad just has some things to do, and I have an appointment. I'll see you guys later." Zoe kissed her head and walked out of the room, leaving them to show themselves out.

Vlad sighed, frustrated with himself. "Let's go, Crystal."

Three days went by before Zoe would take Vlad's phone call. She felt a little guilty, because of Crystal, but she didn't want to talk to him. He'd stepped well over the line with his comment about her being an orphan with a trust fund.

When the phone rang on Friday morning, she finally answered it, letting her annoyance be heard. "Hello?"

"Zoe. I'm sorry."

Silence.

His voice rising slightly, he said it again. "I said I'm sorry."

He's sorry. "Yeah? Me too. Do you have any idea how many people thought that our losing our parents was just a little bit easier because of that damn trust fund? It was like it didn't really count because I wasn't poor. I could almost hear people saying, 'Oh, that's a shame, but she's rich now, so she'll be fine.' What is wrong with you?" Zoe was even more pissed off than she thought. How *dare* he talk to her like that?

"I know, Zoe. I was an ass. I'm sorry. I can't imagine losing my parents like that. And I know what it's like to have people think your life is perfect because you're rich."

"Then why the hell did you talk to me like that? You're supposed to be the one who's always in my corner. You're supposed to be the one who I never have to wonder about. You're *not* supposed to be the one who can strip me bare and leave my emotions hanging out to dry. Not you." Dammit, she was going to cry. She had put her childhood to rest years ago, hadn't she? Much quieter, having lost some of her anger, she said, "You hurt me, Vlad."

"Zoe. God, I'm so sorry. I don't ever want to hurt you. I love you so much. I don't know why I said any of that. I just know that I was angry because you seem to be able to handle anything—and *everything*. I want to be like that. I want to be the one who can comfort my daughter. I guess I'm jealous. I'm so sorry. Please forgive me, moya lyubov. "

Zoe begrudgingly felt a smile tug at her lips. "That's not fair. You know I can't think straight when you speak Russian to me."

"Pozhaluysta, moya lyubov, pozhaluysta prosti menya."

"I don't know what you said, but it's working. I'm going to learn how to speak Russian one of these days so that I know you're not calling me names."

"I wouldn't do that. I'll never take my anger out on you like that again, Zoe. I promise. And I was just asking you to forgive me. In Russian." He didn't know what else he could say.

"Okay, Vlad. I'll try to let it go. Thank you for apologizing."

"Thank God! I was really afraid I'd fucked up beyond repair this time. It won't happen again."

"Okay. So, what's on your agenda for the day?"

"That depends on you. Would you like to go shopping for school clothes and supplies with Crystal and me?"

Zoe knew Vlad didn't want to take Crystal clothes shopping. "Gee, I don't know." She loudly shuffled some papers around so he could hear over the phone. "I have a lot of paperwork to do."

"Please, Zoe. I'll beg if I have to. I don't know what kind of clothes to buy her. And she said she doesn't want me buying her underwear. And she called them 'panties'. I'm her father for Pete's sake! What's the big deal? She's eight. And why does she have to call them 'panties'?"

Zoe laughed. "Vlad, *your* daughter is eight going on thirty. Most of the time, she's not a typical eight year old." Crystal was mature for her age, sometimes too mature.

"Come on. You take her to buy the dresses and frilly shit, and I'll take charge of her clothes for soccer and school supplies. I'll even buy you dinner. Anywhere you want."

"Even if I want to go to The Pub?" Vlad hadn't been to the Scorpions' hang out since he had his surgery. Aside from a couple of get well flower baskets, he hadn't seen anyone from the organization, except Jody.

"I guess it's time to see the guys. Okay, The Pub it is. We'll pick you up in half an hour." He hung up the phone before she changed her mind. Then he called her back.

"Forget something?"

"I love you." He hung up again, and she knew he had that dopey smile plastered all over his face.

Chapter 20

Crystal was animated the whole day. It seemed like each day that went by got a little better for her. Vlad thought that she might even be looking forward to school, because she was getting bored at home.

With the car still packed full of clothes, pens, pencils, notebooks, and soccer gear, the three of them pulled into the parking lot of The Pub. Vlad noticed immediately that the parking lot was full of the players' cars. "Did you call people, Zoe?"

"I might have." She raised her hand to stop him from talking. "Don't get mad at us."

"Us?" He looked at Crystal who immediately looked out the window.

"We thought it would be nice for some of your friends to know that you were going to be here. They miss you. You told them you'd be seeing them, and they haven't seen you in over a month."

"Fine. Let's go in. You ready for this, Little Bit? You're going to meet a lot of noisy people."

Crystal stuck her chin up in that way she did when she was bolstering her confidence. "I'm ready, are you?"

Vlad tapped her under the chin. "If you can do it, I can do it."

After spending a couple of hours at The Pub with his former teammates, it was official. Crystal had each and every one of them willing to cast themselves in front of a bullet for her. Even Cage, who seemed to only care about himself most of the time, was under her spell.

"That was fun. Cage is so cute; he could make you feel better when you're sick just by looking at him." Crystal sighed and leaned her head back against the headrest.

Good Lord, his eight-year old daughter sighed at the thought of Cage friggin' Booker. Zoe and Vlad both turned to her at the same time and said, "Forget it." They smiled at each other as Crystal frowned.

"I'll never forget him. I'm going to marry him someday. You wait and see."

"Over my dead body. Cage is not for you. Besides, he's about a hundred years older than you."

She giggled at him. "I'm good in math, Dad. He's not that much older. He said he's twenty-five. I'm eight, almost nine, so he's only about—she counted on her fingers, "sixteen years older. And he's so cute!"

Zoe took Crystal's side and gave Vlad an innocent smile. "He really is cute, Vlad. Gorgeous even. Maybe too cute for words."

"Yes, that's it, Zoe! He's too cute for words. I want to get a poster of him and put it on my wall, can I Dad?" He was starting to notice that she added 'Dad' in when she wanted something. He had to give her credit; she was good.

"Only if I can use it as a dart board."

They pulled up in front of Zoe's house just in the nick of time. She interrupted their discussion before Vlad got too angry. He still had a chip on his shoulder where Cage was concerned. "I'm going in, guys. I have appointments most of the day tomorrow and some paperwork to catch up on, so let's make plans for Saturday. Is that good?"

Vlad got out of the car to walk Zoe to her door. Crystal followed him, tugging on his sleeve. "Give it to her."

"This isn't the right time, remember? Remember what we talked about?"

"But I can't wait any more. I know you have it. You always have it."

Crystal ran back to the car to get Vlad's jacket from the backseat, while he called after her. "Wait! Crystal! We said—oh, forget it." She was already back, dropping his jacket on the ground.

She looked at Zoe with a secretive smile on her face and a box in her hands, which she gave to Vlad. "Do it. Real romantic like I told you."

Zoe knew what it was, and couldn't help the hitch she felt in her heart. She folded her hands in front of her to keep from reaching out for the black velvet square box.

Vlad rolled his eyes at Crystal. "Zoe, I—"

"Get down on your knee," Crystal said in a loud stage whisper. "Remember? Like the prince."

"It's okay, Vlad. You don't have to get down on your knee." It was one position that still made his hip hurt.

"No, no, I got this." Vlad got down on his knee and started again. "Zoe, I—"

"Daddddddddddy. You're supposed to take her hands. Here, let me show you." Crystal got down on her knees before Zoe and grabbed her hands. "Then you say, Zoe, I love you. I'm sorry I didn't have a ring for you before. And then you say that yucky mushy stuff and kiss her." Crystal smiled at both of them and went back to the car to play a game on her iPod.

"I'm starting to think you rehearsed this, Vlad," Zoe said in a happy tone.

Vlad looked up with all of his love for her showing in his eyes. "I may have once or twice, but there just aren't words, Zoe. I love you and want you to make us complete. We both want you to be our family. I don't want to wait long either, unless you changed your mind and want a big fancy wedding. If that's what you want, that's what we'll do, but—"

Zoe interrupted him by going down on her knees in front of him. She took his face in her hands and kissed him. And kissed him again. And then kissed him some more. When they heard a muttered "gross" they broke apart, grinning like teenagers in the first throes of love. "Can I have my ring now?"

Vlad gave her the box and looked at her face to gage her reaction. He'd know instantly if she liked it or not. He thought she would, but who knew?

Zoe's eyes shone when she looked at her ring. It was exactly what she would have picked out herself. "Oh my God, Vlad. It's perfect." It was a square-cut diamond—set so brilliantly. There was one smaller square cut diamond on either side. Simple but elegant, just like Zoe.

He took it from her and placed it on her finger. "Are you sure you like it? I don't want you to keep something for the rest of your life that you don't love."

"Wow, for the rest of my life. I like the sound of that. I love it, Vlad. Thank you."

"Did she like it?" Crystal yelled out from the car.

"She did!" Zoe yelled back.

"Are you two done kissing?"

"No!" Vlad yelled back.

"Ick."

They both laughed and kissed some more. Vlad pulled away, but Zoe held him close. "You guys should move in with me soon. Assuming you'd rather live here than in a two-bedroom penthouse together."

Crystal overheard her. "Really? Can we, Dad, can we?"

"You hate my place that much?"

"No, it's just that, well, Zoe's place … never mind."

Vlad knew where she was going with her thoughts. "Zoe's place is nicer than mine." He looked at her, trying to encourage her to tell him what she thought.

"It's not that it's nicer, it's just more of a home. I'm sorry."

"I agree with you, Little Bit. Can we move in this weekend?" Vlad would put his place up for sale immediately. He didn't have any emotional bonds to hold him back; it was just a place to live.

"That works for me. Call the moving company."

It turned out that Vlad couldn't get a moving company on such short notice, so he did the next best thing. He called Jody, who called Brandon, who called a bunch of the other guys from the team. He had six guys and two moving trucks within hours of his phone call. Sunday was a down day for the Scorpions, and he suspected that there wasn't much they wouldn't do for Crystal.

It was well after dinner time on Sunday night when they finished hanging the last of Crystal's clothes in her closet. She started school the next day and was understandably nervous.

"You'll be fine, Little Bit. How could those kids not love you? You're nice, friendly, and funny. They'll all want to be your friend." Vlad hoped like hell that what he was telling her would be true.

He found out by eleven the next morning that he couldn't have been more wrong. The principal called him with true concern in her voice. Her tone worried Vlad immensely.

"Mr. Bejsiuk, I'm so sorry to have to call like this."

"What happened? Is Crystal okay?" Vlad was already grabbing his keys off the table. Zoe was with a client, so he quickly scribbled her a note saying he was going out for a little bit.

190

"There was an incident in the girls' bathroom. Some girls found Crystal in there crying. When she told them that she missed her mother, they made fun of her. Then she told them that her mother died, and they began pushing her around and calling her names. I'm very sorry about this. I can assure you, the girls will be dealt with."

"I'm on my way. Is she safe?" Vlad would talk to the parents of these girls himself.

"I have her here in my office with me, Mr. Bejsiuk. I assure you, we will deal with this. I do not condone this kind of behavior."

Vlad got to the school in record time. When he saw Crystal sitting in a chair looking just like she did the day she was dropped off at his place, his heart wept for her. "Crystal."

She wouldn't look at him. She shuffled her feet and kept her head down.

Her feet were wrapped around the metal legs of the blue plastic chair. She wrapped them and unwrapped them. He recognized that feeling of nervous energy—moving just for the sake of having something to focus on. He did something similar when he was in therapy to avoid thinking about the pain.

He slowly kneeled before her and tilted her head up. "Crystal? Are you okay, sweetheart?"

"Yes." She pulled her head out of his grasp and looked down at her feet again, trying valiantly not to cry.

"Come on, I'll take you home."

"Okay."

On the way out, the three girls who had cornered Crystal were sitting in plastic chairs much like those in the principal's office. Vlad wanted to be involved in all steps the school took to punish the girls. "Well, girls, I'll be talking to each of your parents."

"So what? We don't—oh my God." The girl who was speaking poked the girl on her right. "You play for the Scorpions. My dad's a huge fan. We didn't know!"

The girl on her right gasped aloud. "We're sorry, Crystal. We didn't know he was your father."

Crystal, whose chin was nearly glued to her chest, mumbled, "Okay."

Vlad was incensed. "It is *not* okay. None of this is okay. Come on, Crystal." He couldn't remember ever being so mad before in his entire life.

Crystal didn't say a word on the way home, even when Vlad asked her a question. "Honey, you have to talk to me. I want to help you. Those girls, they're not nice, but it has nothing to do with you. I think sometimes people are so sad in their own lives the only way to make themselves feel better is to hurt other people. It's not right for them to do that, but they do."

He needed her to understand that she didn't do anything wrong. *She* wasn't the problem, *they* were. "You're a great person, Crystal. You make people smile and feel good. I know it's hard starting out like this, but it'll get better. You'll meet nice girls and make good friends."

She still didn't say a word. He couldn't blame her. *He* even thought the shit he was saying sounded lame. Who cared what he said? He wasn't the one who would have to go back to school with those nasty girls.

When they got home, Crystal went straight to her room and wouldn't come out again. Zoe couldn't even get her out. "Crystal? We'll leave you alone for a while, sweetie, but you have to come out for dinner later."

Back in the kitchen, Zoe started chopping up peppers. "What are you going to do, Vlad?"

"The school is going to arrange meetings with me and the other parents. Then when I meet them, I'm going to tell them to *control their fucking children!*" He slammed down the pan he was holding, making Zoe jump.

"Jesus, Vlad. You scared the shit out of me."

He didn't even hear her he was so caught up in his anger. He shook the pan in her direction as he spoke. "I can't believe what children are capable of these days. Where are the parents? Is it possible that they don't know what their kids are doing to other kids? I would think *I* would know, wouldn't you? But I've been a parent for all of a week." He slammed the pan down on the counter again and grabbed a fistful of his hair. "This sucks. After all she's been through, she shouldn't have to deal with this too."

Zoe walked over and put her arms around him. "We'll get through it. If it's okay with you, I'll talk to a friend who I went to school with. She majored in child psychology; maybe she can give us some pointers on how to deal with this."

"I'd appreciate that, but can I be on the phone, too? I'd like to hear what she has to say firsthand."

"She actually lives in Orange County. I'll call her and see if we can meet while Crystal's at school. Is that okay?"

"Yes, thank you. Let's get dinner done so we can tag team Crystal and see if we can get her to talk to us." Zoe finished making the salad, while Vlad stirred the spaghetti. He was pouring the spaghetti into the strainer when they heard a loud crash coming from Crystal's room.

The door was just opening as they got to her room and Crystal stepped out. "What was that?" Vlad tried to look past her, but Crystal pulled the door shut.

"Nothing."

"It wasn't nothing, Crystal." He pushed her aside and opened her door. When the scene met his eyes, he had to grab the doorjamb for support. Her room was trashed. The television he had just bought her lay on the floor in pieces. Her beautiful canopy bed was ripped so that it hung down from the frame and there were red spots on it. "Is that blood, Crystal?"

She didn't answer him. She folded her arms, pushed past Zoe and locked herself in the bathroom, momentarily forgetting that there were two doors into the bathroom. "Crystal, let me see you. Where are you cut?" Vlad took her arms and straightened them out. He saw a cut on the palm of her hand.

"It's fine. I cut myself on a sharp edge of my ruler. Just leave me alone."

"No. I won't leave you alone. Why did you trash your room? You loved that bed."

"I don't know. I was mad."

Vlad thought that was rather obvious. "I get that part, but why trash your room? Did that make you feel better?"

Zoe placed her hand on Vlad's arm. "Vlad."

He shook it off and started rummaging through the medicine cabinet for a bandage. "I'll fix your hand."

"No. It's fine." Crystal was in her stubborn mode.

"It's not fine. Give me your hand. Now." To his surprise, she obediently put her hand out and allowed him to bandage it. "Go clean up your room and then come out for dinner."

"Fine."

When she left, Vlad sat down on the tub and looked up at Zoe. "What happened to that sweet, lost little girl? Who the hell was that?"

"She's still that sweet, lost little girl; she's just more lost than sweet tonight."

Somehow they got through dinner and got Crystal's room set to rights. Vlad didn't see a very restful night's sleep ahead of him, and he had a morning meeting with Jody to discuss his position as an assistant coach.

The next day was, thankfully, uneventful. There were no problems at school. Crystal was still quiet and withdrawn. When she got home, she made her way to her bedroom, shutting the door with not much more than a 'hello.'

Zoe let her go. Her friend, Julie, couldn't meet with them until the following week. Zoe gave her some background on Crystal, and Julie assured her that she'd think it over and talk to some of her colleagues to determine what they could do to help Crystal adjust.

Zoe looked up at the faint knock on the door. "Zoe?"

"Hi, Crystal. How are you feeling today?"

"Okay. I just wanted to tell you that I don't want any dinner tonight. My stomach kind of hurts."

Not eating could be a sign of depression, or her stomach might just be uneasy from the previous day. She'd let it go and see what happened in the coming days. "Okay. Did you call Emmy back? She's called twice now."

"No. I will, but I'm going to go do my homework now."

"Do you need any help?"

"No." Then she was gone.

Vlad got home as Zoe was putting dinner on the table. "How is Crystal today?"

"She says her stomach hurts, and she doesn't want dinner. She's in her room, supposedly doing her homework. Emmy's called twice, and Crystal hasn't called her back. So I don't really know the answer to that."

"Okay. I'm going to go look in on her." He kissed Zoe, but when he went to pull away, she grabbed him and kissed him harder.

"I miss this."

"Oh, God. Me too, moya lyubov, me too." Vlad reluctantly pulled away from her. "Keep that thought for tonight. No more putting me off."

"You got it."

Vlad knocked on Crystal's door and pushed it open. She looked at him and tugged on her sleeves. That seemed to be a nervous habit she'd picked up over the last twenty-four hours. "Hi. How was your day today? Did anyone give you any trouble?"

"No. The kids all left me alone today. All of them." She was sitting on the bed with her legs crossed, staring at the flowers on the comforter.

Vlad sat down next to her, and she flinched. He frowned and cocked his head. "Come here, sweetheart." He pulled her into his side, and he felt her stiffen up. "I'm sorry you had another crappy day. It's going to get better, I promise. Are there any girls there that you think are nice? Maybe they're just too shy to approach you."

"Yeah, that's probably it." She continued to stare at the comforter and tugged more on her sleeves. "Thanks. I have some more homework to do."

Vlad rubbed her back and started to question her some more, but thought better of it. "Okay, I'll leave you to it. Are you sure you don't want any dinner? I think Zoe made sloppy joes."

He thought he had her for a second ... "No thanks."

The rest of the week was more of the same, with the exception of Vlad starting to work in his new coaching role. He was taking it easy. His hip was fine with everyday living, but skating was a whole other picture.

"You better take it easy, man. No one expects you to be in top form yet. Don't mess up your hip." Jody was just starting the after-school practice.

"Don't worry about me. Believe it or not, I'll baby this thing. I don't want to undo any of the healing. It feels a little weird, but it's okay so far." Vlad couldn't see very many butterfly plays in his future, but he could live with that.

The kids came out and met Vlad for the first time. There were quite a few starry-eyed gazes in his direction, especially from the girls' team.

"Okay, can I have my goalies down at this end? And some defensemen?" Vlad skated to the far net.

"Forwards and the rest of the defensemen down here with me." Jody split up the defensemen and headed down to his end of the rink to work on stick skills.

Vlad pointed to a girl of about fourteen. "Let's see what you've got. I'm going five hole. I want to see how your butterfly is. Ready?" Before she said yes, Vlad let one fly.

The puck sailed easily right through her legs. Vlad grinned at her. "What's your name?"

"Katie Moore."

"Well, Moore, snap those knees together on the way down. My sheet says you're a butterfly goalie. Everyone will know that and go for your five hole, but don't worry. As soon as you get good at covering that, they'll start going top side." Vlad grinned at her once more as he shot a puck at her quickly that sailed right in again.

"Hey, I wasn't ready."

"Is that what you're going to say when you have a forward bearing down on you? You always have to be ready." He slammed a puck at her again, before he was even done talking. She went down fast and grabbed the puck with her glove, holding it up in triumph.

Vlad gave her a nod of approval as he let another one sail. It went right through her five hole for a fourth time. She laughed, but then got serious and stopped three out of the next five pucks he shot at her. "Good job, Moore. Who's next?" Vlad was going to like his new job.

It rained most of the weekend. It was so rare for San Diego that people actually enjoyed it. It seemed to make Crystal more detached though, if that was even possible.

"Hey, girls." Zoe was trying to get Crystal to play a game with her in the living room, but she just sat there staring out the window at the rain. "You two beauties want to go to the movies with me? I'll even throw in dinner and ice cream. What do you say?"

"Sounds good to me, what's playing?" Zoe asked.

"Can I stay here?" Crystal said at the same time.

"Crystal, why don't you want to do anything? Is school really okay? You keep saying it is, but you don't act like it is." Zoe was getting more than a little concerned with her behavior.

"It's fine. I'll go. Let me get changed." She got up and was out of the room before Zoe could say anything else.

"Zoe, we need to do something. This can't go on. Something isn't right. I mean, aside from what we already know about."

"I agree. I'm going to call Julie again. See if she has any new information for us." Zoe caught herself just before she went into her office to make the phone call. "I'm sorry. How about if you call her?"

"Thanks, but you can call her. I'll see if I can get Crystal to gift me with a couple of words. Maybe even a short conversation." He walked over to Crystal's room and knocked on the door.

"I'm getting dressed."

Well, that was a couple of words. Vlad walked back out to the living room to wait for his girls and have a fun-filled evening, although, he didn't know if that was something they could achieve.

When Crystal emerged from her room, she was again tugging on her sleeves. She was just putting her socks on when Vlad stopped her.

"Crystal, your foot's bleeding." He got up to look at it, but she put her sock on and then her shoe over it.

"I hit my toe really hard on the bed. It's fine."

The evening wasn't as bad as he thought it would be, but it wasn't a fun-filled family night either. They got through it and were home by ten.

Chapter 21

The following week seemed to be going along relatively smoothly. Crystal still wasn't participating in life much, but it was quiet and drama free—and then Thursday rolled around.

It was mid-morning, and Vlad was on his way out the door to pick up some supplies for the hockey school when his cell phone went off. It was Crystal's school principal again. Vlad stared at it for a few precious seconds with a lump in his throat before answering. "Hello?"

"Mr. Bejsiuk. This is Mrs. Parsons again. I'm sorry, but we've had another incident. You need to come down here."

"Another incident? What the hell kind of school are you running?" Vlad was beyond mad. How could his child be in danger at school of all places?

"I understand your anger. I can't tell you how sorry I am. I promise you that I will keep up on this and find a better way to ensure the safety of our students."

"Is Crystal okay? Is she hurt?"

"I'm afraid this was a bit worse than the last time. The girls responsible are being expelled, Mr. Bejsiuk. Crystal is with the nurse now."

He knew there was more. He could tell by the way she kept pausing between sentences. "What aren't you telling me, Mrs. Parsons?"

"They punched her, and they kicked her in the ribs a few times. I'm disgusted by it. Absolutely disgusted. I never would have allowed those girls to stay in school if I believed they would do something like this. I thought we'd seen the end of it."

Vlad's eyes filled. "How could they do that to my little girl? She's just a quiet, sweet little girl. I'm on my way." He hung up the phone and went back to Zoe's office to tell her he was going to pick up Crystal.

Vlad's concern must have been written all over his face. "Oh my God, Vlad. What's happened now?"

He punched the doorjamb in anger. "Those little bitches hit her, Zoe. They punched her and kicked her in the ribs. We haven't even had the meeting with their parents. Well, I'm not waiting anymore. I'm talking to those assholes today!"

"Okay, Vlad, but you have to get a hold of yourself. Let's go down there and see exactly what we're dealing with first. Crystal is the first priority." Zoe grabbed her keys, thinking it would be better for her to drive, and off they went.

Kids filled the fields around the school. Some were playing kickball, some were throwing a football around, and some were just sitting—talking and laughing. It looked like such a happy place. All kids loved recess time, but his child was in the nurse's office with God knew what kind of injuries.

Vlad stormed through the door to the security desk. "I'm Crystal Bejsiuk's father. She's in the nurse's office."

"Follow me, sir. I'm sorry about what happened to your little girl. These kids today are getting meaner all the time. I just don't get it."

They followed him down a long, white hallway lined with lockers on one side. At the last door on the right, the guard motioned for them to go in to the room.

"Crystal!" Her eye was swollen and already showing signs of a bruise. "Oh, honey. I'm sorry. What did they do to you?"

"Nothing. I'm fine."

"What the hell do you mean you're fine? You're not fine! Jesus, Crystal. Tell me what happened."

She shook her head and refused to answer him. The nurse spoke up in her behalf.

"One of the other students saw what happened, but was too scared to stop them. She said that three girls followed Crystal into the bathroom and hit her. When she fell and tried to cover her face, they kicked her in the ribs multiple times. The girl ran to get help then. Crystal's definitely bruised, but nothing's broken."

"Thank you for taking care of her, but I'll be taking her to the doctor's just the same."

"Of course. I can keep her here while you speak to the principal."

At the mention of Vlad and Zoe leaving her, Crystal's head shot up. Vlad was momentarily pleased to at least see her looking to him for reassurance.

"No, she'll go with us. Zoe can sit with her outside the office while I speak to the principal." Vlad gently lifted Crystal off the table and took her hand to lead her away. Zoe noticed that Crystal had wet herself. Without a word, Zoe stopped Vlad and gently took her stockings off of her, so that the she didn't have to walk through the hallways like that. When Zoe kissed her head and gave her a reassuring squeeze, Crystal never even lifted her head.

The principal's waiting room was packed with people. The three girls and their parents were there, along with a boy who was silently crying as his father stared him down. It was a busy day at school.

Vlad stopped in front of the three girls. "You girls happy yet? You get what you needed when you beat my little girl?"

Zoe put a hand on his arm. "Vlad, don't. Let's go in to Mrs. Parson's office and talk about this."

Vlad looked to Zoe and then back to the parents of the girls. "Yeah, let's go talk about this. Let's find out how people raise such vicious, fucking children. You people make me sick."

"That's enough, Vlad. Come on."

Vlad wished he could incinerate those children and their parents with just a glance. To his credit, he did wonder if his violent feelings towards three eight-year old girls might just be over the top. Better that he focused on hating the parents who raised them.

Without preamble, Mrs. Parsons addressed the parents of the delinquents. "As of right now, your daughters are no longer students of Whitman Elementary. They are all expelled for their behavior. You'll have to make other arrangements for their education."

The parents were outraged.

"What?"

"You can't do that!"

"Now, come on, Mrs. Parsons. I'm sure we all agree they need to be punished for their actions, but expulsion? That's a bit much for some schoolroom antics."

Vlad had heard enough. "Schoolroom antics? That's what you call this?" He pointed to Crystal's rapidly swelling eye. "Would any of you want your child to be in the same school with such vultures as your sweet little girls? Do you even *know* what they did to her?" He shook Zoe's hand off his arm and turned to her. "No, Zoe. I need to hear the answer." Turning back to the father who last spoke, he asked, "Do you know what your child did? They cornered her in the bathroom. Three against one. They punched her repeatedly in the face and when she lay down to try and protect herself, they kicked her in the ribs, over and over again. She's bruised all over!"

Only one child had the grace to look ashamed. She started crying, and the ringleader of the three immediately smacked her in the arm. "Stop crying. She deserved it."

Vlad turned on her in fury. "Why? What did she do to you?" The girl wouldn't answer him, so he again addressed her father. "Is this the way you raise your children?"

The mother was the one to speak up. "No, sir, it is not. Believe me; she won't be able to sit for a week when I'm done with her. I'm so terribly sorry this happened." She looked directly at Crystal and apologized to her, too.

The girl looked haughtily into her mother's eyes. "You wouldn't dare. You've never hit me before." She continued to stare at her, arms crossed with her chin raised in defiance.

"Maybe that's where we went wrong, Veronica. Things are going to change, starting today." Veronica's eyes went wide, hearing the truth in her mother's words.

Mrs. Parsons commanded everyone's attention. When it was quiet again, she asked Vlad if he wanted to press formal charges against the girls.

Crystal, who hadn't said a word or made a move since they entered the office, tugged on his sleeve. "Daddy?" she said quietly.

"What, sweetheart?"

"Don't press charges. Can we just go home now?"

Vlad looked at the principal and back at the parents with their children. "I'll think about it." He gathered Crystal in one hand with Zoe in the other and walked out.

Just as they were passing the only girl who had showed some remorse, she reached out to touch Crystal's arm, causing her to flinch away. The girl drew back quickly and whispered with a trembling lip, "I'm sorry, Crystal. And I'm sorry about your mom."

Crystal didn't acknowledge that she'd even heard the girl's apology. It was a case of too little, too late. She tugged on Vlad's hand and kept walking toward the door.

When the three of them returned home, Crystal went directly to her room and stayed there until dinner.

"We have to stop letting her hide in her room, Vlad. I spoke to Julie again. We can let her have time to herself, but she can't be alone all the time."

"I was thinking about that, too. After dinner, I think we should sit her down and make her talk to us. I understand that she might need some time alone to process her thoughts, but she's only eight. She needs to talk to us so we can help her. She needs to know that she can come to me, you know?"

After dinner, which none of them really touched, Vlad suggested grabbing some blankets and sitting out on the deck. The night-time temperature in San Diego only got down to about fifty degrees, so it was rarely too cold to sit outside.

Crystal snuggled herself into one of the lounge chairs while Zoe and Vlad sat in two of the chairs that surrounded the round table, facing her.

"How are you feeling, Crystal?" Vlad started the conversation.

"Fine."

"Crystal, you're not fine. Your eye's swollen shut, you have bruises all over, and you have a cut on your lip." Vlad placed his hands on the table and leaned forward. "Honey, we need you to talk to us about this. I want to know what you're feeling. We want to help you if we can."

Crystal was shifting her legs around and picking at the blanket. "I don't know what you want me to say. Everybody hates me. Hates me!" She kicked the blanket off and stood up with her hands on her hips. "Nobody wants to be my friend. They all talk about me. You don't know what it's like. I hate it here!" She was screaming by the time she was done.

Vlad got up and walked over to her, but before he reached her, she bolted for the door. "Crystal, wait."

She looked at him and then opened the door and ran up to her bedroom, slamming the door hard enough to rattle the windows.

Vlad hung his head in defeat. "Goddammit. How do I get through to her?"

"Well, Julie said we're doing what we're supposed to. We keep talking to her while letting her have some time alone. There's no exact right way, Vlad. We have to figure out what works for her. If it's okay with you, I'm going to see if she'll talk to me."

"Sure, go ahead."

Zoe gently knocked on Crystal's door. "Crystal? Can I come in?" She tried the knob, but it was locked. "Crystal, let me in please." She could hear her banging drawers and thought maybe she was in the bathroom, so she knocked on that door.

"Crystal? I want to talk to you, open the door please."

Crystal swung the door open and went back into her room to sit on the bed, clutching a pillow. "What?"

"I know you're upset and you're not feeling well, but you have to talk to us, sweetheart."

"Why? You have no idea how it is. My mother is dead. That's what all the kids say. I'm a freak because my mother's dead." Tears leaked out of her eyes, but she continued. "They say ... they say ..."

Zoe sat down next to her and put her arm around her. "They say what, honey?"

209

"They say I killed her! They say I'm so stupid and ugly that she didn't want to be here with me anymore, so she died!" Crystal laid her head against Zoe's chest and wept.

Vlad was standing at the door listening, his heart breaking. "Crystal, your mother loved you more than anything in the world. She would have never left you if she had a choice. You know that, don't you?" He walked over and sat on her other side.

Crystal lifted her head up and pushed herself out of Zoe's arms. "I know, but when they keep saying it, I think maybe it's true. They're so mean. I don't know why."

"I don't know why either. But I do know that your mother loved you, I love you, and Zoe loves you. You haven't done anything wrong."

"Do I have to go to school tomorrow? They'll all be even madder at me for getting Veronica and the other girls thrown out of school. I don't ever want to go back!" She flung herself back down on her bed and started crying again.

Vlad knew she needed to go to school, but he didn't have it in him to make her. "No, you don't have to go tomorrow, but you do have to go back. You never know, maybe the other kids will be happier now that those nasty girls are gone. I'm sure you're not the only kid they've tormented."

"No, I'm not. There are a couple of other girls who told me they bother them, too. But they won't hang around with me. They're afraid to." Crystal had stopped crying, but she had the hiccups. "I'm really tired. Can I go to bed now?"

"Sure."

As they were leaving, Zoe cried out. "Ouch!" She looked down and saw a thumbtack sticking out of her bare foot.

Crystal was up in a flash, grabbing the tack from Zoe. "I'm sorry, it must have slipped out of my school bag." She tugged on her sleeves, as was her habit, and hurried back into bed.

Zoe rubbed her toe, watching Crystal hop in bed. "Okay. Goodnight, Crystal."

Vlad walked over and tucked her in. He kissed her on the forehead and told her he loved her. She didn't say anything back and was fast asleep when Vlad checked on her an hour later.

Chapter 22

Sunshine was just starting to peek through the curtains when Vlad rolled over and covered Zoe's body with his. He nuzzled her neck and stroked his hand over her hip.

"Open your eyes." He gave her a nip that had her squirming against him. "Give me some lovin' before the little one wakes up." He ground himself against her, making sure she knew he was ready when she was.

"No kissing."

"Yes, I know the tooth brushing rule. Now, shut up and feel me." He let his hands glide over her, teasing all the way.

"Don't tease me. I've been lying here for almost an hour thinking about you. I'm ready." She shifted so that he was more fully on top of her and spread her legs.

"I love when you do that." He slid deep inside her. "Morning sex is the best."

Zoe wrapped her legs around him and arched her back, silently agreeing with him. She suddenly pushed her hands against his chest. "Stop!" she whispered urgently.

"Why?" he whispered back, slowly moving inside her.

"Oh God. Stop doing that for a second. I thought I heard something."

He stopped but let out a disgruntled groan. "It's too early. I'm sure Crystal's not awake yet." After a minute he resumed his thrusting, but Zoe stopped him again.

"No, Vlad. Stop." She pushed him off her and got up, putting her robe on.

Vlad punched his pillow. "Where are you going?"

"I'm going to check on Crystal. Keep your pants on." Seeing the sheet standing up about seven inches or so, she amended her instructions. "Well, keep your sheet on. I'll be right back."

Zoe quietly tiptoed to Crystal's room and found her still deep asleep. She went back into their bedroom, locked the door, and dropped her robe. "Follow me."

Vlad followed her into the bathroom and watched as she turned the shower on, along with the ventilation fan for some added background noise. She stepped into the shower and motioned for him to follow.

Once inside the shower, Vlad picked her up and entered her in one swift motion as she wrapped her legs around him.

Between gasping breaths, Zoe asked, "Is your hip okay like this?"

"Uh huh." He backed her against the wall and she let out a squeak as she hit the cold tiles. "Sorry," he mumbled into her neck. He squeezed his hands tighter on her ass and thrust harder. All was forgiven.

Zoe was enjoying herself, but she was worried about Vlad's hip. She slowed him down with a hand to his chest and slowly unlocked her legs from him.

"What are you doing?"

"Shhh." She put a finger to his lips and slid the rest of the way down his body. "I think this might be a little more comfortable for you. Believe me, you'll make it up to me."

"Zoe, you know I love—oh God." His hands went right to her head, and his fingers threaded through her hair. "No, wait. I want it to be good for you, too." She kept moving her mouth on him. "God, Zoe. You have to stop. Ah, sweetheart. Fuck, never mind. Don't stop."

And she didn't.

Later that morning, Zoe was cleaning Crystal's bathroom when she came across a strange sight. One of her razors was in the bath tub, and it had blood on it. "Crystal?" Zoe walked out of the bathroom. "Crystal?"

"What?" Crystal was sitting on the floor beside her bed, holding a book, but not reading it.

The pink razor caught Crystal's eye, and Zoe saw a fleeting look of panic move across her face. "Why do you have my razor, and why is there blood on it?"

"I was just playing. I guess I cut myself. It's okay."

"Let me see. Do you need a bandage?"

She moved away when Zoe got closer. "Zoe, I'm fine. I don't know why I picked up your razor. I'm sorry, I won't do it again. Can I finish my homework please? If I have to go back to school, I have to read ten more pages."

Zoe thought that maybe Crystal needed a break from interrogation, so she left her alone to finish her reading. She found Vlad in the kitchen stirring a cup of coffee.

"Hey. I found my razor in Crystal's bathroom. She said she was bored and wanted to try it, but she wouldn't show me her leg. She said she put a bandage on it."

"Where is she now?"

"Still in her room, reading. At least she says she's reading. I don't know that I believe her. Honestly, Vlad. I don't know what to do about her. Everything I read says to give her time. I know she's only been here for a little less than a month, but she seems to be getting worse instead of better."

"I know. I have my last physical therapy session with the ice queen today. I reserved a suite for the Leafs game on Sunday, like we talked about. Tracey's daughter is eight years old, too. I thought maybe she and Crystal might become friends. Who knows? Her daughter goes to a private school. I want to talk to Tracey about that. What do you think?"

"I think if you keep calling the poor woman 'the ice queen', she's not going to want to help you." Zoe laughed. She knew Vlad would have picked Tracey over every other therapist there *because* she was so hard on him.

"You'll understand when you meet her. Wait until you hear her talk about how good the Leafs' goalie is. It's all she talked about. She says his five hole is non-existent; he covers the corners of the net perfectly. It's disgusting. He's not that good. My record was *way* better than his last year."

"Wow, she really does push your buttons, doesn't she? I love it."

Vlad rolled his eyes at her. "Whatever. So, do you think Crystal will want to go? She said once before that she might want to watch hockey."

Zoe thought about it for a minute. "Well, there's a game on tonight. The Scorpions are playing the Red Wings. Why don't we watch that?"

"Okay. Let's make a night of it. I'll bring home crappy, greasy food for dinner. We'll have a party."

"Sounds good. Will you be home normal time or are you setting up teams tonight?"

"I'll be home normal time. Jody wants to wait until it gets closer to our first game to pick teams." They had so many kids sign up for the youth league that they had to form two complete teams. They wanted to make sure the talent was spread between them.

Game night went better than expected. Crystal loved the junk food—mild wings, pizza, and onion rings. She also seemed to be interested in hockey. She especially seemed to be interested in the goal tending. They weren't sure, though, if it was because she knew Cage was in goal or if it could be because she and Vlad were both goalies, although in different sports.

"So, Crystal. I got us a suite for the game on Sunday. A couple of friends of mine will be there, too. They have a daughter your age that will be going. What do you think?"

Crystal tugged on her sleeves as she stuttered, "Do—do I know her?" Crystal was obviously frightened by the idea.

"No, sweetie. She doesn't go to Whitman."

She shrugged her shoulders as if she didn't have a care in the world. "Okay, whatever."

When Crystal turned around again, Vlad shook his head. "Great."

Vlad gave Crystal a Scorpions jacket that he had bought her the day before to wear to the game. It was the first time he'd seen her really smile in days. "Cool."

"Well, let's go." It was going to be strange for Vlad to watch the game from a suite. He didn't tell any of the guys, except Jody, that he was going to be there. He wanted to see how he felt being there the first time.

Tracey, her husband, James, and their daughter, Vicki, met them at the entrance. "Hi, Vlad. You look like you're walking well."

"Yes, thanks to you, ice queen." They made introductions all around and headed up to their suite.

"Wow," James said. "This is quite a setup." They were just right of center ice.

"Can't say I wouldn't rather be on the ice, but it is nice up here. I've sat here once or twice before when I was injured. Help yourself to anything. It's all open bar and all the food you want."

"Sweet. Thanks a lot, man. This is a real treat. I have to warn you, though; Tracey is a real big Leafs fan. She gets pretty vicious when she watches hockey."

"Yeah, well, I'm used to her. She gets pretty vicious if you don't do your exercises to her liking too."

"Only because I care." Tracey grabbed James's arm and headed over to the bar to get a drink.

Vicki was standing next to Crystal trying to get her to talk. "I guess you watch a lot of hockey, huh?"

Crystal was quiet, but she answered her, "I just saw my first game last night."

"Huh? But your dad played for the Scorpions."

Crystal immediately got into her defensive stance with her shoulders back and her chin up, expecting the worst. "I didn't know I had a father until last month. My mom died, and I was sent to live with him." She sounded so angry, Vlad thought Vicki would go right back over to her parents. He was somewhat surprised that Tracey didn't explain the situation to her.

Vicki surprised them both. She put her little hand on Crystal's shoulder and spoke with sincerity. "Oh wow. That's so sad. I'm sorry your mom died, Crystal."

Crystal cocked her head, looking at Vicki in wonder. "Thanks."

"Well, we watch hockey all the time. I can help you learn it if you want."

Crystal let out a shy smile. "Okay."

"Which seats can we sit in, Mr. Bejsiuk? I can show Crystal some stuff while they're warming up."

"We have the whole suite. There are only a couple of other people coming. You girls can sit wherever you want. And get some food and sodas."

Vlad turned to Zoe after the girls had run off toward the food bar before heading down to the first row seats in the suite. "Am I wrong to feel hopeful? Vicki seems really nice. Crystal sure could use a nice friend right now."

"Well, if you're wrong then so am I. They do seem to fit well together. We'll see how the night goes."

By the end of the first period, Crystal was the most animated she had been since starting school. She and Vicki whispered and giggled together like they were old friends. It was as if Crystal was two different people. She really got into the game when Cage got into a fight. Yes, Cage, the goalie.

"Christ, I can't believe this kid." Vlad was horrified. Goalies didn't fight. Well, most goalies didn't fight.

Cage had been doing a great job in the net. With ten minutes left to go in the second period, he had already stopped twenty-eight shots. He'd only let one in, and it had taken a bad bounce off the boards then deflected off one of his own defensemen into the goal. It would have happened to anyone.

Toronto decided to keep things up-tempo by playing their bruiser more minutes than normal. It was obvious they wanted to stir up some shit.

"Why is Ash out there? There's no reason for him to be on that line now. They're up a goal." Zoe looked at Vlad, waiting for his answer.

Miles Ashford was a middleweight enforcer. He tended to play more minutes than a true enforcer, but make no mistake, when this guy was on the ice, you watched your back.

"Not sure. Maybe they're just trying to keep our guys guessing." Vlad pointed to the ice. "Rush is still on the bench."

Carl Rush was the Scorpions' enforcer. He came to the team after Jody retired. He didn't see a lot of ice time, but he did his job well. Seeing him sitting on the bench after the Leafs sent Ash out told Vlad that the coach wanted to keep things quiet.

"Oh, here we go." Vlad was watching Ash during the faceoff. He was pushing up against Marcoux hard enough that he had to scramble to keep upright. Ash had about forty pounds or so on him.

Marcoux shoved back a little, and the ref gave them a warning look as he bent over the centers, ready to drop the puck. As soon as he did, the puck came toward Marcoux, and Ash flattened him into the ice with a cross check right in the middle of his back. He went down hard and painfully, but the ref didn't call a penalty.

Marcoux was ready to go after that, but Ash skated away.

During the same play, the Scorpions were down by their own net, helping Cage defend the goal when Ash pushed their captain into Cage. Lambert fell hard, knocking the net off its moorings, and Cage went bat shit crazy.

He threw off his helmet and gloves and tore after Ash, who was already halfway to center ice. Shouting at him, he didn't give Ash a chance to answer. He simply skated up to him, ripped off his helmet, and grabbed his jersey.

Ash started wailing on Cage so quickly that Cage wasn't even able to get a good grip on Ash's jersey. Cage lost his balance and went down in a heap, taking two hard punches to the head and only delivering one.

"He was lucky," Vlad said. "Ash would've creamed him. What the hell is he doing fighting anyway?"

Crystal spoke up on his behalf. "He was just trying to defend his teammates, Dad. I think he did great."

"Of course you do." *God help me.*

During the second intermission, Tracey gave Vlad the information for Vicki's school. "James is going to talk to the principal for you. He's an architect, and his firm works on the school. He knows a lot of the board members."

"That's really great, Tracey. Thank you. I appreciate it."

"Sure." She looked over at the girls, who were talking quietly, their heads bent close together. "Looks like they're going to be friends."

"I hope so. Crystal could use a friend."

"So could Vicki. She has one best friend, who is also a very nice girl, but that's about it. She was bullied, too, at her last school, and that's why I moved her."

"Really? You didn't tell me that."

"I wanted you to meet her first. I didn't want you to have any ideas in your head about her. If you look at her closely, you'll see that she has a very crooked jaw. It's more noticeable when she talks. That's all the mean kids needed to see. It didn't get as bad as Crystal's did, but I wasn't leaving her in that school."

The girls went into the restroom, but Vicki came flying out a minute later with Crystal yelling at her from inside to come back.

"Mom! Come in here."

Tracey went running into the restroom, with Zoe right on her heels.

Crystal stood there glaring at Vicki. "I told you not to tell!"

Vickie started crying. "I had to, Crystal. I know what you're doing."

"You don't know anything!"

Two fat tears rolled down Vicki's face. "Yes, I do, because I did it, too." She turned around and looked at her mother. "She's cutting herself."

Zoe gasped and went over to Crystal, grabbing her arms. "Where? What? Oh, Crystal. Why?" Zoe was just barely holding back her own tears. How did children get to a point where they had no other outlet than to physically hurt themselves?

"Zoe? Is everything okay?" Vlad called from outside.

Crystal looked at Zoe, silently pleading with her.

"No, Crystal, not this time."

She called out to Vlad. "No, it's not. Please come in here."

"What's going on?" He looked from Zoe to Crystal.

"Show him."

222

Crystal bowed her head and pulled her sleeves up. There were small cuts all up and down her arms. There were some dots, too, that looked like they could have been made with a thumbtack.

"What happened?" Vlad looked completely baffled.

"She did it to herself, honey." Zoe explained briefly about cutting.

Vlad's eyes glistened as he looked from Zoe back down at his daughter. "I'm so sorry, Crystal. God, I don't know what I'm doing with you. I can't believe I let you hurt yourself—that I didn't even know about it. I don't deserve to have you."

Tracey and Vicki left them alone.

Vlad's words broke through to Crystal. Her face was ashen, like she'd been scared witless. "Yes, you do, Daddy. I swear I'll never do it again. Please don't make me leave. Please. I promise I'll be better. Please don't leave me." She flung herself at him, crying so hard he was afraid she was going to hyperventilate.

"Shhh. Oh, sweetheart. I didn't mean I was going to let you go." He continued to whisper to her and rub her back until she calmed herself. "I'll never let you go, Crystal. Never."

Zoe gently rubbed Crystal's head. "Sweetie, tell us why you're cutting yourself. We need to know so that we can help you."

"I don't really know. I just know that I feel a little better when I do. I can't control anything. I couldn't make my mom live, and I couldn't make the kids at school like me." She shrugged. "I don't know."

Zoe thought she understood what Crystal was feeling. She had been reading about bullying, and some of her research explained how sometimes kids felt more in control when they cut themselves because *they* decided when and where to cut. *They* decided how long to let the cut bleed. They felt temporary relief from their pain.

"Honey, you should never hurt yourself. We don't ever want you to be hurt. When you're feeling like that, hopeless and out of control, come talk to us, and we'll see if we can figure something else out together. Do you think you can do that?"

"Yes. I haven't cut myself today at all."

Vlad closed his eyes and clenched his jaw. "You've been doing this every day?"

She looked down and nodded her head. "Mostly after I get home from school."

"Well, you don't have to worry about school anymore. I'm going to enroll you in the private school that Vicki attends."

That news didn't excite her. "Okay."

"I thought you'd want to get out of Whitman."

"I do, but now Vicki knows, and she'll tell everyone."

"No, I won't." Vicki was standing at the door. She walked in and handed Crystal some tissues and a cup of water. "I won't ever tell, Crystal. I promise. I want you to go to school with me. You, Marissa and me will be best friends forever. It's a nice school and you'll love Marissa. She's a nice girl."

They had missed most of the last period and decided to call it a night. Tracey pulled Vlad aside before they left.

"She'll be okay, Vlad. Vicki will be a lot of help to her. I know you want to be the one to 'cure' her, but Vicki understands how she's feeling better than we do. You'll see. She's going to be fine."

"Thanks, Tracey. For everything." Vlad reached around Tracey and shook her husband's hand. "I'll call the school on Monday."

Chapter 23

The next night Crystal cut herself once again. Zoe and Vlad were curled up in front of the fire when Crystal came out to find them.

"Hey, Little Bit, what are you doing out of bed?"

Crystal looked up at him with a flood of emotions in her eyes. She looked haunted. He hated that look.

"Come here, sweetheart." He picked her up and sat her on his lap, even though she was a bit too big. "What's wrong?"

She pulled up her sleeve, exposing a tiny new cut. "I cut myself again. But then I stopped and came out to talk to you."

Vlad pursed his lips together to keep himself from yelling. *Shit.* "Okay, well, I'm glad that you're coming to me now. Why did you do it?"

"My mom's birthday is next week. And … I don't know. I'm just … I …"

Oh my God, her mother's birthday is so close to Christmas. This kid can't catch a break! He put his hand on her head and pulled her up against him, trying to give her some comfort. "I'm sorry, Crystal. I didn't know, honey." He got an idea. "Why don't get a cake and celebrate her birthday? We can do it every year."

She pulled her head back to look up at him. "Can we? I'm so scared I'll start to forget her."

"You won't forget her. I won't let you. We'll make it a tradition. We'll have cake and look at pictures of the two of you. Does that help a little?"

"Yeah. I'm still sad, but it's okay. Thank you." She kissed him and slid down off his lap. "Dad?"

"Yeah?"

"Thanks for keeping me."

"I love you, Crystal."

She looked back at him and said quietly, "I love you, too."

Vlad thought they may have been the sweetest words he'd ever heard.

It had only taken Vlad a couple of days to get Crystal enrolled into her new school. It was the second time he threw his name and money around to get things done, but he wanted to get her settled and into a daily routine as quickly as possible.

"Even though there's nothing I wouldn't do to help Crystal, I still feel dirty buying her way into that private school. It's wrong that other kids don't have the same opportunities she has just because I can pay for it and they can't."

Zoe had just shown her last client of the morning to the door and was enjoying a cup of coffee with Vlad at the kitchen table. "I know what you mean. It *is* wrong, but that's the way things work. Maybe we could set up some kind of scholarship at the school. Between the two of us, we certainly have the money to sponsor it."

"That's what I love about you. You're always thinking of ways to make things better for other people. I'll make an appointment this week to speak to the head of the school about setting up a scholarship fund."

"You know, I've been thinking about something else. What would you think of me changing my profession a little?"

"Huh? To what? I thought you loved your job."

"Oh, I do. I don't mean taking on a completely different occupation, I'm thinking of 'hanging up my skates' so to speak and concentrating on child psychology. I want to help kids like Crystal. Who knows? Maybe I could even help the kids who do the bullying figure out a better way to deal with their own emotions. There's got to be a way to stop the bullying cycle."

"Zoe, I think whatever area of psychology you choose to work in will be all the better for having you in it. You know I'll stand behind you no matter what you do. I think it's a great idea. I can't stand thinking about what Crystal went through—is still going through. It's not fair."

"That's another thing I've been thinking about. From the research I've done, children who start cutting as young as Crystal, tend to fare much worse than children who start in their teens. I want to make sure I know all of the signs to look for. I want to beat the odds with her. And I think we can."

Vlad reached across the table and took her hands in his. "I hope we can, sweetheart. I'll do anything to beat the odds. At least we know she hasn't cut herself in a while. It's a start, right?"

Zoe had been checking Crystal weekly to see if she had any new cuts. She was doing well, and even seemed to like the structure of the weekly exams. It was as if the weekly checkups were giving her something that she could control. She was proud when she showed Zoe there were no new cuts. "It's a start, absolutely. I just don't want to get too relaxed and find out she's going in the wrong direction again."

"I know what you mean. It's scary to think that she could go back to being that sad little girl who was hurting herself. We just can't let it happen." Vlad looked at his watch and got up from the table. "Since I have the day off, I'm going to go do some Christmas shopping and then pick Crystal up from school, okay?"

"Sure. I think I'll call Julie and see what she thinks about my idea to switch specialties. I'm sure she'll have some pointers for me."

As Vlad got up, he looked down at Zoe and caught a glimpse of her breasts in the V of her blouse. "On second thought …" He picked her up out of her chair and sat her on the kitchen counter.

"Oh, I like the way you think." Zoe spread her legs and pulled him into her with her hands on his hips. "We haven't done it on the counter yet, have we? Thank God for granite." She slapped her hand down on the surface. "Nice and strong. Unyielding."

Vlad glided his hands up inside of her blouse, caressing her belly on his way up to cup her breasts, eliciting an appreciative moan from Zoe. He unclasped her bra and gently pinched her hardening nipples, watching her eyes as he did so. "I love to watch you when I bring you pleasure." He continued his leisurely assault on her breasts until she, not so gently, yanked on his hair to pull him close enough to reach his mouth.

Zoe plunged her tongue past his lips in an effort to feel a deeper connection to him. She continued to kiss him until his hands came down to roughly grip her hips and tug her off the counter. He immediately began undoing her pants and slid them down her legs, kissing every beautiful inch of her skin on the way down.

"I could taste you all day, do you know that?" He tossed her pants to the side, but left her high heels on. He really had a thing for her in high heels. Not bothering to take his time, he ripped her panties off and buried his face in her, tasting the sweetness that was uniquely Zoe.

"Jesus, Vlad." She said in a whoosh of air. "Slow down, baby, you're going to make me come."

With a low growl, he continued to lick her as he freed himself from the constraints of his jeans. Just as he felt the first subtle tremors from deep inside her, he stood up, lifted her back onto the counter and entered her fast and hard.

She threw her head back as the pleasure from his hard, quick thrust went through her body. Getting leverage by placing her hands behind her on the counter, she tilted her hips down slightly and thrust her hips back toward him. She felt instant gratification at the new angle.

Vlad continued to slide in and out of her until he felt her tightening up. "That's it, Zoe. Feel me fucking you."

"Yes. God, I love the way you fuck me."

He grabbed her hips harder, knowing he'd leave marks, but also knowing she wouldn't care. She liked his hands on her.

"Harder, Vlad."

He gave her what she needed. "Come for me, Zoe. Come for me now." He was about to lose the battle he'd been fighting with his own release, but he wanted her to come first. "Ah, God, Zoe. I can't ..." With a roar, Vlad came hard and was happy to feel her squeezing around him as she reached her peak and tumbled over it.

As Zoe's muscles slowly stopped contracting around him, he pulled her gently off the counter and sat them in a kitchen chair, still joined. He cradled her head in his hands. "We are so good at that, moya lyubov."

"I will never get enough of you, Vlad." She traced the line of his jaw. "You are so gorgeous. I mean seriously hot. And the inside matches the outside. I'm a lucky girl."

Crystal was doing very well in her new school, and had become fast friends with Vicki and Marissa. She was finally acting like a contented eight year old girl.

The celebration for Crystal's mother seemed to put her further at ease. Vlad had contacted Thaddeus, who was only too happy to put a DVD together of pictures for her.

Even though it made her cry, Crystal loved watching that DVD. During Carla's birthday celebration, she sat glued to the TV as she ate the birthday cake Zoe had bought. It had been almost two months since Carla had died. It would take much longer for the pain to dissipate to an acceptable level, but she was making progress.

"It's so good to see her." She looked to Vlad, who also had a suspicious sheen to his eyes. "I miss her so much. Thank you."

Vlad wasn't sure if he was helping or hindering by giving her all of those pictures to look at. He hoped he was doing the right thing. Time would tell.

Chapter 24

Crystal was noticeably happier by the time Christmas Day rolled around. He knew he owed a lot of that to her friendship with Vicki and Marissa. The three girls were inseparable.

Christmas Day itself was a quiet affair. It was just the three of them—and Izzy. Jody and Lacey had gone to Vancouver to spend the holidays with her family so they were taking care of their dog. Crystal was in her glory, and Zoe could see a dog in their future.

After all of the dishes were washed and put away from Christmas dinner, Crystal asked them when they were getting married.

"We were thinking about getting married on Valentine's Day, but remember, it's going to be a small service and then a big party."

"Can I still wear a pretty dress? And hold flowers?"

Zoe smiled at her. "Of course. How about something in pink?"

"I like pink."

Crystal went back to playing with her new toys and throwing Izzy's rag doll for her over and over again, as Vlad sat there looking at them, thinking how lucky he was. It was his best Christmas to date.

As time went by, Crystal became acclimated to her new life. She was learning to be happy again. She still had melancholy moments, but to their knowledge she'd only cut herself again on that one occasion that she had told them about.

With Crystal in bed for the night, Vlad gathered Zoe up in his arms as they sat in the overstuffed chair, staring at the fireplace.

"Did you ever think we'd get here, Zoe? You and me, an eight-year-old girl, and a huge beast of a dog lying at our feet?"

"No, but keep in mind, the dog's not staying." She turned and kissed his cheek. "I love you, Vlad Bejsiuk. I know I gave you a lot of grief, but I'm glad you kept interfering in my life."

"I had to. Sometimes interference gets the girl."

Epilogue

It was a beautiful sixty-five degrees the day of the wedding. Zoe, Lacey and Crystal were at the courthouse waiting for Vlad and Jody.

"You look gorgeous, as usual, Zoe." Lacey held her hands and looked her over. "Red is such a fabulous color for you."

Zoe looked at Lacey's huge belly and felt a stab of envy. "No, *you* look gorgeous, Lace. Huge, but gorgeous." Zoe was the only one who could get away with telling Lacey how big she was. "I'm a little jealous."

"It'll be your turn soon enough."

Zoe looked around to make sure Crystal hadn't heard her. "Shhh, I told you, I'm not sure. I haven't said anything. I only just missed my period."

"Go buy a test! What are you waiting for?"

"I just don't want to be disappointed. I figure this way, it can kind of sneak up on me, you know?"

"Well, I can't wait to have Addie. I'm tired of being pregnant. Three more weeks. Ugh, I don't know if I'll make it." Lacey looked around the room as if in search of something.

"What are you looking for?"

"I thought I heard Jody's truck. He always has food on him, and I'm hungry."

Zoe was laughing as Crystal tugged on her skirt. "Zoe?"

"What is it, sweetheart?"

"I'm hungry, too. When is Daddy going to get here?"

"Well, if you two weren't so superstitious, he would have come with us. Now, you have to wait."

"That's my fault. Jody's late for everything."

No sooner had Lacey spoken then Vlad and Jody walked into the waiting room.

Vlad marched right over to Zoe and took her in his arms. "You look beautiful. How did I get so lucky?" He loved that she was wearing red. He couldn't have even imagined her in a traditional white wedding gown.

Zoe's vows were very traditional, but said with heartfelt emotion. To Zoe's surprise though, Vlad had made his own vows.

"Moya lyubov, I'm not good with words, you know that, but I want to try." He cleared his throat and rubbed his thumb over the back of her hand as he spoke.

"From the first time I saw you through the glass at your front door, I wanted you for my own. I chased you for years. I drove you crazy. I made you angry. I made you happy. I made you sad. I made you laugh, and I've even made you cry. But none of those things compare to what you've done to me." He got down on both of his knees before her, taking both of her hands in his.

She looked down at him with tears in her eyes. "What are you doing?"

He smiled up at her. "Shhh. It's still my turn."

She obliged and didn't say another word.

"You've made me rethink the way I live my life. You've made me rethink what it truly means to be a man. You've taught me the right way to love a woman. You've shown me that my heart is no longer my own—I share it with you and Crystal. You've made me strive to want to be the best husband I can." He looked over at Crystal and winked at her. "To be the best father I can." His voice rough with emotion, he finished his vows. "Zoe, I love you with everything I am. I swear to you that I will try each and every day to be worthy of the love you've given me. For the rest of my life, I will be thankful that you're my wife. YA lyublyu tebya."

Zoe sank down to her knees in front of him. "I love you, too." She wiped her tears away and kissed him.

"And they lived happily ever after." Crystal said. "Just like the princes and princesses do."

The End

Please turn the page for a sneak peek at
***Cage's Misconduct.* It is subject to change.**

CAGE'S
MISCONDUCT

Cage loved wedding cake. People usually turned their noses up at it, but that was his favorite part of a wedding reception. He had a big sweet tooth, and he was lucky he was an athlete or he'd be one huge man.

He was strolling around the hall at Vlad & Zoe Bejsiuk's wedding celebration looking for his conquest of the night. He was getting tired of redheads. It wasn't that he didn't like them—he'd had a bunch of redheads over the past six months or so—but it was time for a change.

He was just about to stroll up to a leggy blonde standing by the door when he caught a flicker of something ice blue floating by. As he turned to look, a bunch of the guys from the Scorpions walked over to where he was standing. He hardly even noticed them. His gaze was riveted on the blue dress.

Karen was so excited to be there. She hadn't spent much time in San Diego before. She'd only been there for a couple of quick visits. This time, though, she was there to scope out job opportunities. She was ready for a change and wanted to move to San Diego permanently.

Being surrounded by so many hot hockey guys could be exhilarating, but she'd be cold, dead, and buried before she became just another notch on a bedpost. There was nothing wrong with having a little fun, but she was over that. She was twenty-eight years old and wanted to find Mr. Right. She doubted she'd find him amidst a bunch of rowdy NHLers, although they were fun to hang around with from time to time.

Taking a break from making small talk with everyone, she wandered over to the bar. "Can I have a dirty martini please?"

Keith Lambert, the captain of the Scorpions snapped his fingers in front of Cage's face. "Yo. What are you looking at? Hello? Booker?" Keith looked over to where Cage was looking. There were too many people standing around to pick out who he was looking at, but then the crowd thinned.

"Booker. Hey man, listen to me. Not her. Do you hear me? Not her. Anyone else in the entire room, but not her."

"Are you crazy man? Look at the tits on her. And Christ! Her ass is more than a handful. Yeah, I'll be having me some of that."

Keith looked behind him and cursed. "Cage, I'm telling you, man, shut your mouth."

"Too late," boomed a voice that Cage belatedly recognized.

Jody LaGrange, all six-foot-three, two hundred thirty pounds of him, was the former enforcer for the Scorpions, and he had always hated Cage, but never more than at that moment. He whipped Cage around and planted his fist so hard in his face, the bone breaking sounded like a clap of thunder.

"What the fuck, old man? You broke my fucking nose!"

"Keep your goddamn eyes off my little sister!"

Acknowledgements

My first acknowledgement goes to Beth MacMullin. She is an awesome beta. She always makes time for me and gives me detailed notes. I can run ideas by her and know that I'll get an honest answer, even if it's not what I want to hear. She's priceless.

I also want to thank my awesome cover designer, David Goldhahn. I think he outdid himself on this cover. It is gorgeous!

Thank you to Madison Seidler for her editing. I still haven't quite figured out those commas!

And a special shout-out to my Facebook followers. You guys/gals are awesome. You're so supportive, and I love when you bug me for a release date! Thank you!

You can connect with me via the web at here:
https://www.facebook.com/NikkiWorrellAuthor
https://www.goodreads.com/author/show/6950511.Nikki_Worrell
www.nikkiworrell.com

CPSIA information can be obtained at www.ICGtesting.com
Printed in the USA
BVOW06s0724091016

464549BV00020B/649/P